# TRULY, MADLY, *sweetly*

## A SWEET LOVE STORY

# KIRA
# ARCHER

Entangled Publishing, LLC
2614 South Timberline Road
Suite 109
Fort Collins, CO 80525
Visit our website at www.entangledpublishing.com.

Lovestruck is an imprint of Entangled Publishing, LLC.

Edited by Erin Molta
Cover design by Heather Howland
Cover art from Deposit Photos

Manufactured in the United States of America

First Edition April 2016

*As always, to my hubs and the kidlets.*
*And to Tracie Bush, for letting me borrow Street Treats for a*
*little while.*

# Chapter One

Natalie checked her mirrors, held her breath, and eased her truck out of the parking space at the depot. She waited for an opening in the traffic whizzing by — a delicate operation that was sometimes more than her frazzled nerves could take. She loved Hoboken, loved being so close to New York City, and was thrilled she'd finally managed to save enough to get her own food truck (scratch that — mobile cupcakery). But the traffic...the traffic she could definitely do without.

Navigating the delicate ecosystem of food truck vendors was harrowing enough. They were angry that she, a relative newcomer, was getting a prime location. The only reason they hadn't run her out of town was because the lady she'd bought the truck from had taken her on as a sort of informal apprentice the year before she retired. Since Natalie was more or less taking over the woman's cupcake business, the other vendors grudgingly considered her grandfathered in. Well, at least the bitch-outs were down to once or twice a week rather than every day. Yay for improvements!

The blaring honk of the truck behind her jolted her out

of her ruminations and she punched the gas, lurching into the flow of traffic, holding her breath until she made it safely onto the narrow street. Gina, her BFF and sometime business partner, was so much better at the driving thing.

Unfortunately, Gina had had a hot date last night and was still MIA, so Nat had to wing it on her own through the incessant honking horns and wall-to-wall moving metal death traps. Give her a nice, safe train any day.

Then again, the food truck allowed her to peddle her delicious wares all over the city and hopefully, she'd be able to make enough to buy her own bakery one day. A real storefront, maybe in a gorgeous old brick building...with a green and white striped awning over the door like the one her dad used to take her to on her birthday every year. The daydream kept her company while she made the drive to the PATH and pulled into her sell spot, a prime place across from the busiest exit of the train station. All those harried Wall Street drones disembarking from their busy day jobs were always jonesing for a good sugar rush. And the moms and nannies ferrying kids between activities and shopping trips were generally good for a sale, too. Business had been amazing.

Not to mention, she was parked right next to the gelato truck which allowed her to indulge in her favorite pastime: ogling one particular suit who had a serious addiction to the frozen stuff. No matter what the weather, if the gelato truck was there, her heavenly hunk of blond deliciousness never failed to stop by for a cone. One day she'd rev up the nerve to try and convert Mr. Gelato from ice cream to cupcake— maybe.

Natalie popped open her windows and set about straightening the mess that Gina had left the night before. She rearranged the selection of cupcake toppings in alphabetical order, her shoulders relaxing a bit once everything was back in its proper, logical, and organized place. She made sure the counters gleamed, the cupcakes were displayed in the most optimum way, and she was ready for her first customer. The other vendors glared good morning at her and she smiled sweetly back. She'd win them over…eventually.

Gina showed up three hours later, bounding into the truck in a sickeningly good mood. "Sorry, sorry, sorry!"

"I had to drive," Nat pointed out.

"I know, totally my bad," Gina said, wrapping the neon pink and green apron with their Street Cakes logo emblazoned on it around her waist. "I'm amazed the truck is still in one piece."

Gina ducked and the cupcake Nat threw at her bounced harmlessly off the wall. "Your aim seriously sucks."

Nat snorted. "Tell me something I don't know."

"Go take a break. I'll hold down the fort for a few minutes."

Nat grinned and grabbed a bottle of water. A nice little stroll did sound good. "Just for a minute. Don't burn the place down while I'm gone."

"I'll try." Gina stuck her tongue out, the little girl gesture looking totally out of place with her favorite heavy eyeliner, lip ring, and pink streaked black hair. "Get out of here."

Nat stepped outside the truck and took a deep breath, lifting her face to the slight breeze. The end of summer had given way to slightly cooler days, but it still got uncomfortably hot inside the truck. She closed her eyes and took another good breath and stepped around the side of the truck onto the sidewalk.

Right into a man who'd been innocently enjoying a cone of chocolate gelato.

Her forehead collided with his elbow…the elbow that was attached to the hand that held his cone…the cone that had been lifted to his mouth…the cone that was now plastered all over his face and, from what she could tell, was also lodged a good way up his nose.

The gorgeous, perfectly sculpted nose that belonged to her Mr. Gelato.

"Holy crap! I'm so sorry!" Nat turned around and grabbed a handful of napkins from the ledge of her truck, throwing a horrified glance at Gina who was staring with her jaw hanging open.

"Here," she said, trying to mop up his face.

He hadn't moved or said a word and Nat worried that the gelato had somehow made it so far up his nose it had frozen his brain and paralyzed him. She opened her mouth to apologize again when he suddenly lifted a finger, his face screwing up into a horrible grimace. He snatched the wad of napkins from her and she jerked back. But instead of throwing them in her face as he had every right to do, he brought them to his own face and sneezed. Explosively.

Nat gasped and turned back to grab another handful of napkins, thrusting them into his dripping hands.

He took them, nodded his thanks, and blew his nose several more times.

"Here." Gina tossed her the baby wipes they used for sticky situations and Nat turned back to Mr. Gelato, who seemed to be doing much better now that he'd cleared his sinuses of the frozen treat.

"I'm so, so sorry. I didn't see you there."

One corner of Gelato's mouth quirked up. "Obviously."

Nat gave him a hesitant smile and handed him the wet wipes. He mopped his face off and cleaned up his hands before getting as much of the goop off his shirt as he could.

"You missed a spot," Nat said, reaching up to wipe a bit of chocolate from the tip of his nose. He didn't move but stood still, watching her with a pair of unbelievable blue eyes. Almost gray. Like the color of the sky just before a storm, when it should be too dark to see anything, yet the sun manages to shine through. The ring surrounding the iris was such a dark shade of gray it was almost black. The combination was striking.

Nat also couldn't help but notice her head would fit perfectly into the hollow beneath his chin. And she bet it would feel pretty damned wonderful to have his arms wrapped around her, arms that were encased in a gorgeous tailored suit. If the straining seams were any indication, they were probably everything her imagination was cracking them up to be.

His smile grew wider, showing a row of straight, white teeth. A tiny scar cut through his upper lip just at the right corner. She had an outrageous urge to kiss that spot. She bit her own lip instead, trying to get a grip.

"I think you've gotten it all," he said. "Might have taken off a few layers of skin, too."

Nat blinked and dropped her hand, her face flaming hot. She'd been standing there dabbing at his face like some hypnotized monkey. He must think she was totally insane. She took a big step backward, hoping he realized she came in peace, despite the mess she'd made of his beautiful shirt.

"I'm so sorry," she apologized yet again. "You have to let me pay to get your suit cleaned. Here." She snatched a business card from her back pocket and thrust it into his hand. "Just call me and let me know how much it is. I, ah…"

He still stared at her with a mixture of amusement and something else she couldn't quite pinpoint. At least he wasn't screaming at her or threatening to sue or anything. Though the scrutiny made her squirm. She decided she'd better cut her losses while she could and make a quick getaway.

"I gotta go," she said, suddenly wanting to be anywhere else but there. "Sorry again!" she called over her shoulder.

He looked like he was going to say something but she

didn't stick around to find out what. Gina could continue to watch the truck. Nat needed to get a good, solid grip first. She turned to scurry off as fast as her unfashionable, but comfortable, orthopedics could carry her.

. . .

Eric hurried inside his brownstone, flipping on the lights. He tossed his ruined shirt onto the couch, a smile on his lips at the thought of Cupcake's face when she was mopping him up. She'd looked perfectly edible. That delicious, kissable mouth hanging slightly open, those gorgeous hazel eyes wide with surprise, curls as deep brown as the chocolate he loved so much, escaping the bun she had them tucked in. He'd seen her around town in that crazy pink and green truck, but he'd never been big on cake so he hadn't stopped. He might have to rethink his position on that particular dessert.

"Pathetic," Jared said. His friend trailed in and stood staring at him, his face puckered in disappointment.

Eric looked over, his brows raised in surprise. "What?"

Jared shook his head. "Some crazy chick ruins a shirt that cost more than I make in a month and you're just standing there with a dumbass grin on your face like you're happy about it. You should be suing her for damages, not trying to figure out the best way to ask her out."

"I haven't asked her out."

"Yet."

"Yet," Eric agreed.

Jared shook his head, picking up the shirt. "She's trouble, man. Usually they end things by destroying your shit. I wouldn't want to find out how this chick ends things if this is how she starts it." He chucked the shirt at Eric who caught it effortlessly.

Eric grinned. "You only say that because you haven't met

them with twin expressions of shocked horror.

"What?" Nat asked Gina. "He was helping my bee sting."

Gina eyed Eric up and down. "Uh-huh, that's what it looked like he was doing."

Eric thankfully ignored her and turned to Random who was wearing such a smugly knowing look that Nat wanted to slap it off his face.

"Natalie, my friend Jared. Jared, this is Natalie." Eric made the hasty introduction, giving his friend the knock-it-off-dude glare while he did.

Nat bit back a smile and introduced Gina who just nodded at each of the guys, her mouth still puckered in a slight frown. Gina wasn't the most trusting when it came to men.

Eric led the way out of the truck and they went to inspect the damage she'd done. Natalie groaned inwardly. She'd apparently cranked the wheel while being attacked and her bumper had shaved a nice strip of paint from the driver's side door and his side mirror hung at a weird angle.

"I'm so sorry," she said, reaching out to straighten the mirror. "I'll pay for all the dam—"

The mirror snapped off in her hand and she stared at it in horror. "Shit."

Eric's laugh echoed through the air and Natalie looked at him in surprise.

"It's okay," he said, taking it from her. "It's just a mirror and a little paint. No big deal. I was thinking of changing the color anyway."

"I'll pay for it, I promise." She wasn't sure how, but she'd make sure she did. She snagged another business card from her back pocket. "Here," she said. "In case you lost the one from earlier. Call me and we can get it all arranged. I'll call my insurance company and…"

"That's okay. We can handle it between ourselves. No need for anyone's premium to get raised over this."

"You are being so nice about all this. Really, most people would have torn me a new one."

Eric laughed again. Natalie liked his laugh. Deep and throaty, no holding back. His smile transformed his face from that of a sculpted Norse god into something infinitely more human, a bit softer maybe, and sexy as hell.

"Maybe I just like being nice to pretty girls."

Natalie snorted. She'd seen her reflection in the broken mirror. Her cheek was red and slightly puffy, her mascara had run a bit, ringing her hazel eyes like some sort of cracked-out raccoon, and she was pretty sure she'd seen a few sprinkles lodged in her always errant curls.

Her suspicion was confirmed when his hand snaked out and plucked something from the top of her head. He looked at it closely for a second and then licked it from his finger.

She'd never wanted to be a finger so badly in all her life.

"*Hmm*. Chocolate. My favorite."

Natalie opened her mouth to reply and couldn't, for the life of her, think of a single thing to say. All the blood in her body seemed to have evacuated her head to pulse hotly south of the border. She seriously needed to chill the hell out.

Eric flashed that heart-melting smile at her again and rubbed his finger over her card. "How about I give you a call later tonight and we can set up a time to discuss everything. Maybe over dinner?"

Was he asking her out? No way did he just ask her out. Did he…

Eric laughed again. "It's just dinner, Natalie. Nothing major."

Natalie smiled. "Okay," she said, trying to feign a calm sense of cool that she was far from feeling.

"Good." He lifted a finger and gently touched her cheek above the sting that she'd almost forgotten about. "You take care of that."

"I will."

The sound of her phone blaring from her pocket snapped her back to reality. She hurried to shut off the alarm, cutting off Black Sabbath's "Iron Man" (chosen in honor of His Royal Studliness Robert Downey Jr., not out of any allegiance to the gods of rock and roll).

Eric grinned. "Great song."

"Sorry," Nat said. "I always double alarm so I'm not late."

"I'm actually late, too."

They both turned toward the bakery and took a step, stopping and looking at each other, asking simultaneously, "Are you…?"

Gina and Jared looked between the two of them.

Jared snorted. "Well, this'll be fun."

# Chapter Three

Nat knew Gina would give her a hell of a time over the whole accident fiasco, but all thoughts of that disaster faded in the face of the miracle that had just occurred. Nat stared, dumbstruck, at the best thing that had ever happened to her. It was beautiful. Nothing more than a dirty strip of concrete really, but the rickety doors that had hidden it from view opened to each side and beckoned her like a pair of outstretched arms. Natalie clutched the ownership papers in her hand. "It's mine? Really?"

Mr. Davis, the lawyer for old Mrs. Lambert who had owned the building Nat lived in, gave her a vague smile. "Yes, Miss Moran. Well, the parking spot. The building adjacent to it was left to Mr. Schneider." He nodded at where Eric stood leaning against his car, thumbing through a sheaf of papers Mr. Davis had given him.

"Wait, what?" Nat asked. "I inherited a garage but the building it's attached to belongs to someone else? How does that work?"

"That's something you'll need to work out with Mrs.

Lambert's nephew."

Nat frowned, more confused than ever. She hadn't known Mrs. Lambert had a nephew. And who in the world inherited a parking spot? Well, a garage really. She swallowed her disappointment over the loss of the building. It looked like an old bakery and Nat had seen a glimpse of stainless steel through the windows, a good sign there were appliances inside.

That building would be the answer to all her prayers. It must be the bakery that Mrs. Lambert had run years before, a shared love they had bonded over during their frequent chats. She hadn't known Mrs. Lambert still owned it, though. If it *had* been a bakery in some distant past and was still zoned and licensed for it, it could mean a prep kitchen all of her own. She wouldn't have to keep renting the microscopic kitchen she currently shared with four other vendors to store her ingredients and bake her cupcakes. Or better yet, an actual storefront — of her own.

Maybe Eric would let her rent the space. Having her prep kitchen adjacent to where she parked her truck would be a dream come true. Though hell, even with the parking space alone, Mrs. Lambert had just given her a luxury very few vendors could afford. A luxury that was only four blocks from her apartment. It was too good to be true. If Eric was amenable to the idea. He might not be so thrilled that the garage didn't go along with the building. Then again, he worked on Wall Street, so what use would he have for an old bakery? Maybe she could broach the subject when they went out. If he still wanted to go out. Though, damn. She didn't want him thinking she was only going out with him because she wanted the building.

The lawyer continued, breaking into the haze of thoughts flooding her head. "If you'd like to sell it, I can take care of that for you. Of course, according to Mrs. Lambert's will, you must give Mr. Schneider first rights on buying the garage. And vice versa, if he wants to sell the building. But if he declines, you'll have no trouble at all finding a buyer. The parking spot alone would bring you a lot of money."

Gina perked up, pushing off from the cement wall she'd been leaning against. "How much?" she asked. Nat frowned but Gina just smiled and shrugged. "I'm curious."

"I oversaw the sale of a client's spot in the depot down the street for eighty grand last month. With an actual private garage like this, you could probably get more. Quite a bit more."

Nat's mouth dropped open.

"Holy crap," Gina said. "Nat…"

Natalie was already shaking her head. As much fun as the money would be, she wanted the space more. It would save her more than it was worth within a couple years with the depot fees she would no longer have to pay. Not to mention, if she could get Eric to let her use the kitchen, she'd save on prep space fees also. And if she could get the whole building… "So, if I wanted to buy the building, how much would that cost?"

The lawyer shrugged and handed her another sheaf of papers and a pen. "That would be up to Mr. Schneider. The building hasn't been used in some time, so it might be possible to get a good deal on it. For a building of this size in this location though, I'd say a minimum of $350,000. As for the garage, just sign here, here, and initial here, and it's all yours."

Anxiety roiled in Nat's stomach and threatened to evict the cupcake she'd chowed down for dinner as she debated her chances of getting Eric to sell for a buck. That's about all she could afford. No way could she scrape up the fortune the building would cost. Not while she was still paying off her new food truck, which could probably use a trip to the body shop now. And that wasn't even considering the repairs on Eric's car. And his shirt. She was going to pay for those, no matter what he said.

She scrawled her name on the papers, her signature looking nothing like her usual graceful letters, and smiled. Despite everything else, excitement rippled through her. This spot was going to make her life so much easier and save her serious cash!

"Congratulations," Mr. Davis said, with all the enthusiasm of a cat facing a water hose. "Oh, this is for you as well." He handed her a sealed envelope.

"What's that?" Gina asked.

Nat opened the envelope and pulled out a single sheet of paper covered in Mrs. Lambert's shaky script.

*My dear girl,*

*A slab of concrete might seem an odd gift, and odder still to leave the bakery to someone else, but I can think of no one who will put it to better use. Get that truck of yours rolling and spread some sugary cheer around this cranky old city. Your visits and cupcakes were the highlight of my days. It does my old heart good knowing that I can help you start your business. And perhaps a little something else, as well.*

*Thank you for bringing a little light into my life.*
*Franny Lambert*

Nat blinked back tears. She'd always made it a point to stop in and say hi to Mrs. Lambert, usually bringing her a leftover cupcake or two after she'd finished selling for the day. She hadn't realized it'd meant so much to the sweet old lady.

Nat had always done decent business, but the fees at the shared kitchen she rented and the parking fees at the depot were killing her profits. It took a lot of sales to keep her in the black. With this spot, she wouldn't have the depot fee. And if she could rent some kitchen time from Eric, she'd be able to get some sleep instead of having to bake in the middle of the night (which, at the moment, was the only time she could get into the kitchen she time-shared). Plus, she would save herself from having to lug trays of cupcakes up and down three flights of stairs to her apartment in Mrs. Lambert's old brownstone, where she had to store them until the next morning when she started selling.

Figuring out where to park her truck at night had been a constant source of anxiety. The depot she was in was pricey, crowded, and prone to vandals and break-ins. Her truck had been graffitied twice already. But she'd been determined to make it work. Her fears over her apartment, at least, had been alleviated with a letter from the new owner, a Mr. Schneider, Mrs. Lambert's brother. And Eric's father, apparently. He'd inherited the building with the stipulation that Nat got to keep her apartment at her current rent at least for the length of the new five-year lease she had just signed. And now, thanks to Mrs. Lambert, Street Cakes had a place to park its wheels at night. But what did Mrs. Lambert mean, *starting something else, as well*?

A tinge of suspicion trickled through her but before she could voice it, Gina grabbed her arms and jumped up and down, dragging Nat along with her. That was all it took to unleash the excitement that had been cautiously building inside her. They squealed like they hadn't done since they were in high school. Nat knew they looked like complete dorks, but for once, she didn't care. Her dreams had just possibly come true. Sometimes a little girly squee-fest was called for.

Male laughter froze Nat in her place. Her muscles clenched against the familiar flutter that hit her every time she saw him. By now she should have a rock-hard six-pack going on. At least then she'd get something out of this daily torture. And experiencing him up close was so much more intense than viewing him from afar through the window of her truck. Maybe he used that pheromone soap from those commercials. If he did, she was going to write up a ringing endorsement on Amazon. Because it was *working*.

Eric strolled over to her, standing a little closer than was socially comfortable. Nat's body nearly purred.

"Hi." She inwardly cringed at the lameness of that single syllable, especially since it made no sense for her to say it. But it was either that or let on how hot she was for him. And she'd rather carve out her own heart and hand it to him on a gilded platter than let him in on that little secret. At least for the moment. It had been a big enough day, as it was.

"Hi," he said, his lips slowly stretching into a sexy smile that Nat could picture waking up to after a night of crazy sex. His blond hair was slightly damp. The sudden image of him naked and soapy in a steamy shower made Nat's vision go fuzzy around the edges.

She bit her lip and focused on breathing. Gina leaned over and whispered in her ear. "Watch yourself, your orgasm is showing."

Nat gasped, her heated cheeks making the bee sting throb anew.

Eric, his forehead creased in thought, turned to Mr. Davis. "So, despite the odd breakup of the property, there should be no impediment for me to reopen the bakery, is there?"

"The building is yours to do with as you'd like, Mr. Schneider."

"What in the world are you going to do with a bakery?" Gina asked Eric.

Before he could answer, Jared butted in. "What she said. What the hell are you thinking?"

Eric shrugged. "I don't know. I loved this place as a kid. It'd be a kick to start it up again."

"You don't even like cake," Jared pointed out.

"You can sell more at a bakery than just cake. Maybe I could specialize in Italian pastries or something. I like those," Eric said.

Jared snorted. "Sure."

Nat couldn't do more than stare at him as her dreams shattered with every word out of his mouth.

"Seriously?" Gina said. "No offense, but what are you doing thinking about selling Italian anything? You're a blond guy named Schneider, for shit's sake. Shouldn't you be frying up crumpets or strudels or something?"

Eric chuckled. "Really? What does my name, or hair color, have to do with — "

"*Ahem.* If there are no further questions...for me," the lawyer said, frowning at Gina. "I've got a meeting in the city."

The lawyer slid the papers Eric had just signed into his briefcase, handed both Nat and Eric a card, in case they wanted to discuss selling their respective properties, and took himself out of the garage as fast as his Italian loafers could carry him.

Jared turned back to Eric. "Are you seriously thinking about opening this place up again?"

"Why not? I've wanted to start my own business for a while. I hadn't thought of a bakery, but it would be a great investment. Especially if I already have the building and at least some of the equipment."

"Yeah. You could. Except for the minor fact that you know absolutely nothing about baking. Like at all."

Eric scratched his chin, rubbing a finger over the stubble cropping up on his skin. "It's really not a bad idea," Eric muttered to Jared. Nat narrowed her eyes at him but he ignored her and kept thinking out loud to his friend. "The biggest upfront expense of starting a business is always the basics. And if the basics are literally being gifted to me, I sure as hell don't want to waste the opportunity."

"You could just sell it off, use the money for something else," Jared suggested.

"Maybe. I like the idea of building something of my own, though. And when is the next time I'll have this kind of chance? It's not every day someone just hands you everything you need to start up a business."

Jared shrugged. "I still think a bakery is the wrong biz for you. Besides, you know your parents will flip if you turn baker boy."

"They'd get over it."

Jared snorted. "Whatever, man. They'd disown you in a heartbeat and that's a lot of damn money to give up, just for a chance at being Betty Crocker."

Nat stood watching them spitball back and forth, like she wasn't even standing there. Another second of listening to them flushing her dream down the toilet and she was going to scream.

Eric didn't answer for a minute, then shook his head. "Well, I guess they'll just have to get used to the idea."

Jared's eyebrows rose and Eric grimaced at him. "I mean it. I couldn't do what I really wanted and go to art school. And yeah, they might have had a point with that. Not many lucrative job opportunities in the art world. But this is something that might work for both of us. I can do something a little more along the lines of what I've always wanted to do. It's not painting, but it's creating, of a sort. And it's a real business, something that my aunt was very successful at, so there's every reason to believe I can make a success of it. My parents can hardly complain if I'm a successful business owner."

"Yeah, I think they were thinking more Wall Street tycoon and less Martha Stewart."

"Whatever. Martha Stewart is more successful than my dad will ever be. I could aspire to a lot worse things."

"If you say so."

"I do say so. My aunt had this place hopping. She was a total self-made success and that's something I've always wanted to do. Not that my dad hasn't worked his ass off. But I've never had any real interest in his business. There's just something appealing about actually building a business from the ground up. Dealing with the day-to-day struggle of it. Being face-to-face with your customers. God, I can still smell the pastries my aunt used to have in this place. I'd love to resurrect it. I bet she's got some recipes in her files somewhere. I could sell all the stuff she used to sell. Biscotti, cannoli, and oh my God, she made the best sfogliatelle. And we've got to do baklava too. I could eat that stuff for days."

"Minor detail, dude. You have no fucking clue how to make any of that shit you just mentioned."

Eric glanced over at Nat and she tried to clear her head of the buzz that had filled it since Eric had started spouting off, so she could hear what was coming out of his mouth.

"Maybe you could help me," he said to her. "Just get it started, I mean. Maybe show me how to bake a few things. Can't be too hard."

Her mouth dropped open and Gina laid a hand on her arm, whether to comfort her or restrain her, she wasn't sure.

"You can think about it for a minute, if you need to."

"Gee, that's big of you," Gina said, glaring at him.

Eric ignored her. He and Nat were left staring at each other, each holding a newly signed stack of papers that branded them stuck together…unless one or the other could come up with a crap ton of cash. And Nat knew her position on that one.

Eric shoved his papers in his back pocket. The tip of the bundle caught his shirt and hiked it up a bit, exposing a sliver of skin just above the waist of his jeans. He wandered around her new parking spot. Nat's eyes lingered on that smooth expanse of skin, momentarily thankful for his apparent love of soft, old jeans that sat low on his hips. If the cord of muscle she saw as he walked was any indication, Eric was hitting the gym fairly frequently. Realizing it had been quite a while since she'd been to the gym herself, she suddenly wished she hadn't pounded down that cupcake quite so fiercely that evening.

"Well?" he said, turning around and catching Nat's gaze on him. His lips twitched knowingly and Nat scowled, trying to will the blush out of her cheeks. It didn't work.

"Well, you have the building, but I need the garage," Nat pointed out.

Eric paused, a slight frown creasing his forehead. "Look, not to sound rude or anything, but why did my aunt leave something to you, especially something like this? How did you even know her?"

Nat's eyes widened and she bit back her first defensive response. It was a reasonable question, she supposed. "She was my landlady. And my friend."

"You were friends with your eighty-six-year-old landlady?"

"Yes, I was." Her throat tightened.

Eric's eyes narrowed, fixed on her as if he were trying to figure out if she were telling the truth. She held his gaze. She had nothing to hide. Visiting with old Mrs. Lambert had been a pleasure for Nat. She was going to miss her.

Finally, Eric gave a brief nod and looked around the garage again. "Well, I guess I'll just buy you out then. How much do you want for it?"

"Hang on. First of all, according to the lawyer, spots like this can go for eighty grand, minimum."

Eric's jaw dropped. "Are you kidding me? It's just a garage. Eighty grand—"

"Actually, more like twice that. At least. Eighty grand is apparently the going price for a regular parking spot. Not a whole garage. Which is irrelevant, because there is no way I'm selling. Sorry, but I need this spot."

"Since I now own the building this garage is attached to, it makes sense that I own the garage, too."

"That might make sense to you, but I don't want to keep paying the crazy fees at the depot. I need this spot. I'm not selling."

"Look, I have no idea what my crazy aunt was thinking of splitting the property up like this. But I'm sure I can get enough—"

Nat shook her head, all visions of smearing him head to toe in frosting quickly melting away. "Sorry. I need this spot more than I need the money."

"Well…" He sighed and jammed his fingers through his hair, making the usually spiked tips of his faux hawk stick out in odd directions. "We can't both use the spot."

"I realize that."

"Look, I know it would be more convenient for you to have a private parking spot, but if I'm going to restart this bakery, I need that garage. If I can offer expanded parking for my customers or even delivery, it would increase my chances of success—"

"Yeah, well, keeping the spot so I don't have to pay the astronomical fees at the depot means a lot more than just convenience to me." Nat took a deep breath, her anger building with every word out of his mouth. "Actually, I wanted to see if you'd consider renting the building to me, or at least some kitchen space to me for my prep work…"

"Except I plan on using that kitchen space for my bakery."

"Your bakery that you just decided to open five minutes ago? Your bakery that you don't have the first clue about operating?"

Eric folded his arms and Nat tried not to notice the way his biceps strained the seams of his soft cotton shirt. "Well, we're right back where we started, aren't we?"

Nat let a little smile peek out. "Looks like it."

She stared at him, unable to think of anything else to say. She wasn't going to back down. She needed this spot. He stared back at her, probably thinking the same thing. He needed it too...which meant they were sort of screwed. And not in the good way.

"You could share it."

Nat, Eric, and Jared all turned to look at Gina, triplet expressions of surprise on their faces.

"And how exactly would that work?" Jared asked.

Gina turned to Nat and Eric. "Since neither one of you is willing, or able probably, considering the price, to sell, you don't really have a choice. Maybe Nat can make your deliveries for you in exchange for some kitchen time. That way Nat doesn't have to keep renting the shared kitchen she's been using and you get to offer catering without having to get your own truck."

Jared piped in his two cents. "And maybe she can teach you *something* about baking while she's at it, since you really don't have a clue."

Eric shot him a dirty look but didn't fight the suggestion. He opened his mouth like he was about to argue, but after a second he shut it, his forehead crinkling. Nat also tried to think of an argument against Gina's idea. And failed. Sharing the garage and the kitchen would mean a lot more interaction with Eric, a thought that had her squirming at the thought of all the awkward encounters in her future. She ignored the part of her that was jumping for joy at their forced involvement. No good would come from letting that bit come out to play.

Nat met Eric's gaze and after a moment he shrugged. "I'm game if you are. I haven't got any other ideas."

"I guess it could work. But if I'm out making deliveries for you, I won't be operating my truck, which means I'm not making any money."

"But you won't be losing any money on parking fees either. And it's not like you'd be in the bakery all the time. It probably won't take long to show me what I need to know. I'm sure you can still run the truck, at least part time."

"I can take a few more shifts for a while," Gina offered.

"I guess…" Nat said, still not convinced she wasn't getting the short end of the baguette.

"I won't be catering every day. I was thinking of starting off slow, anyway, not catering really, just offering deliveries for larger purchases. And for those, I should have advance notice when I'll need you. So I really shouldn't be taking too much of your time. But just to sweeten your deal, how about I pay you for whatever time you spend making deliveries for me. In exchange for some crash course lessons in running a bakery."

Nat slowly nodded. Kitchen time and payment for occasional deliveries in exchange for a few baking lessons. No depot or shared kitchen fees. "All right. Deal."

"Well then." He stuck his hand out and Nat stared at it for half a second before taking it. His skin was warm and smooth against her own and she resisted the urge to close her eyes and wriggle in delight at being able to touch him again.

"Co-owners?" he said.

Nat nodded. "Co-owners. For now."

"Mamma Mia" blared from his pocket again. He let go of her hand. "I better get that. We'll work out the details later, okay?"

Nat nodded and watched him walk out the doors. Jared grunted. "Later." Gina glared at him. But Nat caught the way her friend's gaze lingered on his well-formed backside. She hid her smile. Gina could never resist a challenge. Neither could she, it seemed.

"Oh, and Nat," Eric said, poking his head back around the corner.

Nat jumped. "Yeah?"

"You still owe me that dinner." He gave her a crooked smile and ducked back out.

She didn't realize she was smiling back until she caught Gina's raised brow. Nat cleared her throat and looked down at her shoes.

"Well…this'll be interesting," she said.

Gina snorted. "Understatement of the year, my friend."

# Chapter Four

Eric rang Natalie's buzzer and prayed she'd answer. He was nearly an hour late. He couldn't help it, but still, making a bad impression with her was the last thing he wanted to do.

Instead of buzzing him in, she opened the door and stepped out on the stoop.

"You're late."

"I know, I'm sorry," he said. "My parents were having drinks with a few prospective investors and insisted I be there. I left as soon as I could."

Natalie's forehead crinkled in a slight frown. "They have these really cool devices nowadays that allow you to call or even just send a message to someone instantaneously."

Eric rolled his eyes. "Yes, Madam Sarcasm, I'm aware. My father has strict rules about keeping phones out of sight when schmoozing investors."

"Daddy said no?" she asked, a slight smile on her lips. "All righty, then."

The look on her face shouted loud and clear what she thought of his excuse, but explaining further would probably just sound worse. She shoved her hands into the pockets of the black cardigan she wore. His gaze raked over her outfit: a simple skirt and blouse with the cardigan, a pair of black boots. She looked amazing. She'd probably look amazing in anything. But the outfit was safe. Nice, but not too nice. Dinner with a friend nice. Not romantic date nice. Which was fine since they weren't on a date-date. But…disappointing.

Eric shoved his hands into his own pockets and tried to push away the thought of what she might be wearing if this *was* a real date.

"So, where are we going?"

"Ah, it's a surprise," he said, grinning. "Luckily, I was able to pull a few strings and get our reservations changed."

He held out his hand and Nat hesitated just a moment before taking it. He wrapped his fingers around her hand. It fit perfectly in his.

Half an hour later, Eric sat across from Natalie at one of the most upscale restaurants in town. It would blow his whole paycheck to pay for dinner but, well, he'd wanted to impress her. And make up for showing up an hour late. And, if he was honest with himself, to butter her up. He might need her help to get the bakery up and running, but he really needed that garage. The happier he kept her, the easier it would be to get her to sell.

He didn't seem to be doing a great job though. Natalie had squirmed all through the appetizers, barely touching the oysters Rockefeller. He couldn't really blame her. They were supposedly delicious but they looked like something that belonged in a tissue, not on a plate being sold for thirty bucks a serving. The whole point of the dinner had been so they could iron out the details of their little arrangement. That, and he just wanted to spend time with her. Not that she needed to know that. Yet. Maybe ever. But they'd barely spoken more than a dozen words to each other.

Right. Time for a game change.

He crumpled his fine linen napkin and laid it over his plate. "Let's get out of here." He was instantly rewarded by a dazzling smile that made her eyes light up like warm caramel. He slapped a fifty on the table that would cover the appetizers and drinks they'd ordered and took her hand, leading her out into the warm night.

As soon as they were outside, he let go of her. He'd rather have pulled her closer and wrapped an arm about her waist, but they were nowhere near that stage. And probably never would be if they couldn't get the whole inheritance thing figured out.

"Sorry. I'd heard this place was great."

"Oh, no. It was fine. Really."

He smiled down at her, grateful she was trying to spare his feelings, but not fooled for an instant. "I do know a great spot just down the street. I promise it'll be better than this."

Nat aimed a skeptical glance his way but nodded. "All right. Lead the way."

Five minutes later, he watched with growing amusement as her eyes widened in surprise when they stopped in front of his favorite dinner place.

"Mack's Mystery Meats?" she asked.

"Best sausage sandwiches anywhere in the city."

"Buffalo? Wild boar? Alligator?"

"All very lean and extremely healthy. And tasty," he promised.

"So where does the mystery come in?"

"If you're feeling brave, you order the Mystery Meal and Mack will surprise you with something wildly exotic you're guaranteed to love. It changes every week. I ordered it once and got kangaroo."

"What?" Her expression said *OMG* but she couldn't hide her curiosity, faint as it might be. One side of her mouth quirked up into a little pucker that was so adorable he chuckled. "Or you can stick to the menu. They have regular old beef and chicken for those who aren't feeling so adventurous."

Her lips relaxed into a smile. "Oh, good. What do you like?"

"The elk is my favorite, but they are all good."

"You've tried them all?"

"Yep. All very tasty."

"I hate to be a total drag, but I think I'll stick with a regular hamburger and fries for tonight."

"Well, maybe I'll be able to talk you into trying a bite of my sausage."

She swallowed, her cheeks blushing a bright pink. He opened his mouth to say he'd so not meant that to sound the way it did. But on second thought…he kept his mouth shut. Trying to fix it would just make it worse. Might as well go with it. He gave her what he hoped was his best smoldering look.

Nat snorted. "I think we'll hold off on that for now."

Eric smiled. Whatever. She was squirming again, for a much more enjoyable reason. He liked her reaction. Very much. Too much. As much as he'd love this date to lead to a little pleasure, he needed to keep it all business. Maybe later, after everything was all worked out. This damned bakery business was going to ruin his sex life.

He ordered their meals, boring hamburger for her, elk flavored with apples, pears, and wine for him. They walked for a bit until they found an open bench. For a few moments, they ate in comfortable silence, saying nothing as they chewed and watched people walk by. He'd never just sat with a girl before, not feeling the need to fill the silence. But it was actually nice to just relax.

He glanced at Nat and found her staring at his sausage roll. His eyebrow rose a notch.

"Wanna try it?"

She shook her head and went back to picking at her fries. "No, thanks."

"Ah, come on," he said, picking up the sandwich and holding it out to her. "Chicken?"

"No, it's elk. That's the problem."

He laughed. "You know what I meant."

She grinned. "Maybe. Still not sure about that," she said, waving at the sausage.

"I promise, you'll love it. It's not really that different from beef. A little sweeter maybe. Not gamey at all, especially the way Mack cooks it. And just in case," he grabbed a napkin and held it up, "I'll have this ready to go if you need to spit it out."

She leaned forward a bit, a slight frown creasing her forehead. "Gimme the napkin," she said, taking it and holding it open in the palm of her hand. "All right. Just a tiny taste."

Eric brought the sausage up to her mouth, sucking his breath in with a tiny hiss when she wrapped her lips around it and bit down. He closed his eyes and forced himself to breathe. He needed to get a grip. She'd taken an innocent bite of his sandwich, not shoved her hand down his pants, but his body couldn't tell the difference.

He watched while she cautiously chewed, her napkin in one hand, a bottle of water in the other, ready to rinse the taste from her mouth if needed. Instead, her eyes widened a little in pleased surprise.

"Told you," he said, taking another big bite himself.

"It's not bad," she admitted. "Not sure I'm ready to try kangaroo just yet, but the elk is pretty decent."

"*Um-hmm,*" he mumbled around a mouth of food.

They took a few more minutes to finish their dinner and then Eric gathered up their trash and tossed it.

"Want to walk?"

"Sure," she said, getting up.

"So," he said. "You're cool with your friend's suggestion?"

"Yes," she said, but the slight frown creasing her forehead was back.

"But?"

She glanced at him for a second before turning her attention back to the scenery around them. "No buts. It's a good solution. For now."

"For now?"

She shrugged. "I could use the kitchen space. It'll save me a ton of money on renting time in a shared kitchen. And it will be a lot more convenient to prep near my truck in my parking spot."

He didn't miss the slight emphasis she placed on those last few words but ignored that for the moment.

She continued. "And I don't mind helping you get things up and running and making a few deliveries in exchange for being able to use the kitchen."

"But?" he asked again.

"However…" she said with a little smile, "what happens when we've got the bakery going and you've got your own truck for deliveries and some staff to help you keep it running and don't need me around anymore? Am I out of a kitchen or do I still get to use the facilities?"

Eric thought for a second. It was true, once he was set up he wouldn't really need her help anymore. But it would be kind of a dick move to totally kick her out on her ass. Besides, maybe being generous with the kitchen space would help with the whole garage issue.

"I don't see why you can't keep using the kitchen when the bakery is closed."

"What would you charge me?"

The fact that she didn't even try to get him to let her use it for free both impressed and bothered him. He found it admirable that she didn't expect to get something for free but at the same time, he didn't like that she assumed the only way he'd give her access to the kitchen once their arrangement was over was if she paid. It was a reasonable assumption, though, so his feelings on it made no sense at all.

He waved her off. "We can discuss all that later. It will probably take a few months to get the bakery in decent shape. Plenty of time to work out the kinks on what happens once it's running."

Before she could protest, he moved on. "It's going to take several weeks, at least, of full-time work to get this thing going. Can you take that much time away from your truck to do that? I don't want you to risk your own business to get mine going."

She blinked, seemingly surprised at his concern. "I've got it worked out with Gina. She'll run the truck full time for a few weeks until I get you going. I'll still help with the baking and morning set-up and if she needs me during the day, I'll be close."

"That's nice of her."

"I don't know what I'd do without her. She's an angel."

Both of Eric's eyebrows hit his hairline at that one.

"Not how you'd describe her?" Nat asked, her wide smile showing a slightly crooked tooth that was probably the cutest thing about her.

"Angel? No. She seems a bit on the scary side for an angel."

Nat's laughter rang out, drawing more than a few admiring glances. Her laugh ended on a little inhalation of breath that was somewhere between a squeak and a snort. It was the most adorable thing he'd ever heard. Spending a couple months trying to keep his hands off of her was going to kill him.

"Gina's not so bad. She came up with this whole crazy idea, remember?"

Eric snorted. "I guess even Satan's Mistress has her good moments."

Nat gave him a playful shove. Before he could respond she turned and nodded at a building. "This is me."

He looked up in surprise. He'd been so focused on Nat he hadn't even realized they'd arrived.

Nat nodded. "You didn't come here often, did you? I never saw you."

Eric shook his head. "When I saw her we'd usually meet somewhere for lunch or dinner."

He let his gaze roam over Nat again. So this was the girl that his aunt used to go on and on about. Her inheritance of the garage was making more sense. His aunt hadn't mentioned that Nat had been her tenant. But in the last couple of months she'd mentioned a certain young lady of her acquaintance with increasing frequency. He hadn't really been listening.

But he'd heard enough to know that Nat had been very kind to his aunt. His estimation of her went up even further. There weren't a lot of people left in the world who'd take the time to keep an old lady company. Natalie had meant a lot to his aunt.

"What?" Nat asked, looking down at herself, as if she were trying to figure out what he was looking at. The woman had no clue.

"Nothing," he said, smiling down at her until her cheeks blushed that delicious shade of pink again.

She cleared her throat and broke eye contact. "So, when do you want to get started?"

He thought for a second, quickly going over what he'd need to do to get the bakery opened up. "It'll probably take me a week or two to get everything lined up and ready to go. Give my boss some notice."

"You're quitting your job?"

"Not just yet," he said with a grin. "But I've got a ton of

vacation time and some personal days I can bundle together. I'll have to make sure my clients are covered for a few weeks though, finish up a few things."

"Okay. Well then, when do you want me?"

*Now. Here. Repeatedly.*

Eric swallowed the words and looked away from her while he got himself under control. Amazing how a simple little question could throw him from adult conversation straight into horny teenager territory.

"Let's say a week from Monday, meet me at the bakery at eight a.m.?"

She hesitated a second, apparently doing some mental calculations of her own. "That will work. I guess I'll see you then."

Eric nodded, but hung around a second, not exactly sure how to say good night. A handshake? That seemed lame. A hug? Probably too friendly since it was technically just a business meeting. Something a little more friendly than that would be fantastic, but was definitely out of the question. And still…he didn't want the night to end just yet.

"You know, it's still early. Why don't we go out and celebrate?" he asked, before the idea had fully formed in his mind.

"What?"

"Come on," he said, warming to the idea. "Both our dreams just got made, or mostly so. Let's go celebrate, toast a few to my crazy old aunt."

"Gina's probably waiting up for me…"

"Bring her along. It was her idea for us to work together."

Nat still hesitated, but Eric could see her wavering.

"Come on. There's no way I'm sleeping for a while. Might as well dance." He grabbed her hand and spun her around, startling a laugh out of her. "Go grab your girl, I'll call Jared, and we can go celebrate our mutual good fortune."

Nat laughed again. "All right. Give me a few minutes."

She bounded up the steps and disappeared into her building.

Eric whipped out his phone and called Jared, who was, of course, up for a party. Then he planted himself on the stoop to wait for Natalie.

This arrangement was going to be interesting. Excitement at getting the bakery going had been a constant hum beneath the surface since he'd signed the papers making it his. He damn near vibrated with it. Like a kid on Christmas Eve, too amped up with anticipation to sleep. He'd wanted his own business for a long time. Something that was his, that he could build from the ground up. His chance to leave his mark, make his own success.

The prospect of spending some quality time with Natalie enticed him even more. And that was a problem. She was off-limits. At least until everything was all said and done. Until then…he needed to keep his mind on business.

Starting tomorrow.

# Chapter Five

Natalie grabbed her tequila shot and raised it above her head. "To Aunt Franny!" she yelled over the thumping tones of Pitbull.

Eric, Jared, and Gina raised their glasses, echoing her toast and clinking their glasses before knocking back the shot. Nat shook her head and swallowed, shivering a bit as the liquid fire burned its way down her throat, warming her chest and loosening her up one molecule at a time.

She slammed her glass on the table. Her body pulsed in time with the music, the beat thrumming through her. She jumped up and grabbed Gina's hand. Gina grinned at her and Nat backed up, leading her onto the dance floor, her hips already swaying to the beat.

Nat studiously avoided looking at Eric. He lounged back against the booth bench, one ankle hooked over the other leg, one arm draped over the back of the bench, his glass dangling from his fingers. They'd stopped at his place on the way to the club so he could change and pick up Jared. Her mouth had been watering for him since he'd jogged down his steps, tight shirt tucked into low-riding jeans, black leather jacket doing nothing to hide his absolutely delicious body.

Her head spun a little. She wasn't drunk, but she'd had enough that the edges of her world were delightfully blurred. Under normal circumstances, she'd never feel confident enough to go out on a dance floor in front of a hot guy and shake her assets like they were worth something. But the alcohol gave her a self-assurance she hadn't felt in a long time. Not since before her jackass of an ex, Steve, had used her, stolen her work and claimed it as his, and dumped her. She still cringed whenever she saw that cookbook. Which was all the time, since the damn thing had been endorsed by Rachel Ray, featured on her show, and had hit the bestseller list. Skyrocketing Steve's career. A career he wouldn't even have if it hadn't been for her writing the entire book in the first place.

It was supposed to have been theirs. Together. Apparently, Steve had had other plans....

She shied away from that thought and focused on the music thrumming through her and the delightful way the nerve endings in her body sparked and tingled. Another shot or two and her inhibitions would be completely gone. Better cut it off now. No telling what she'd do if Eric got within ten feet of her.

Natalie spun around, her long curly hair flying as she twirled. She very seldom wore it down. The riot of curls that hung halfway down her back were usually pinned into a tight bun or ponytail when she worked. And she was always working. But for tonight, her hair was loose and free. And so was she.

Nat grinned at Gina, who was doing her best Miley Cyrus twerking impression. And she was doing it pretty damn well, actually. Nat laughed and closed her eyes for a second, letting go of everything. The song playing blended seamlessly into one of her favorites. She let out a breath.

"Sing it Fergie," she murmured. The woman was right…a little party never killed nobody. And Nat was damned determined to enjoy herself. She just got a garage. For free. In New Jersey, no less, which meant she could actually use it to park her food truck, unlike in New York. And kitchen time in the attached bakery, in exchange for a few hours of her time teaching a gorgeous hunk of a man the ins-and-outs of a bakery. Life could definitely be worse.

Nat let loose and shook her ass for all she was worth. The worries she'd been hauling around slipped away. She forgot about everyone else on the floor and just danced. Her blood pumped through her system, heating her skin, leaving her breathless as she spun.

Nat could feel Eric's eyes on her, burning into her, through her. She glanced at him, meaning only to take a quick look, but her eyes locked with his. She turned to fully face him, letting her hands roam down over her hips, her thighs and then slowly back up. Into her hair, lifting it and letting it fall free again. Part of her couldn't believe what she was doing. The other part couldn't believe it had taken her so long. She'd been fantasizing about her Gelato Man for weeks. And by some miracle, he actually seemed interested in her, too. Even if it *was* just the alcohol talking. No way was she going to waste the moment. She bit her lip and swayed her hips again, keeping her eyes locked on his.

The corner of Eric's mouth slowly lifted. He threw back the shot in his hand and stood, coming toward her. He'd taken off his jacket and his shirt clung to him, letting her see every minute movement of his body as he began to dance. He reached for her, pulling her into him, his hand burning through the thin fabric of her dress. Nat pressed her hands against his chest, her breath catching in her throat at the contact she'd been craving all night.

He drew her in, molding their hips together in a quick grind, before pushing her away, spinning her around, and wrapping an arm around her waist. Her ass nestled firmly against his hips, they swayed, their bodies glued together, pulsing through the slower bridge of the song. The alcohol buzz had nothing on the effect of Eric's hands on her, his body moving with hers. Nat hazily wondered if it were possible to pass out from sheer lust.

The tempo slowly picked up and Eric spun her around again. Nat laughed, grabbing his hand, moving with him in time to the bass that thumped through the club. She didn't know where Gina was. Didn't care. Didn't see anyone but Eric, didn't feel anything but his hands on her body, his breath against her neck when he pulled her in close.

A slower song blended through the speakers and Eric drew her into his body without skipping a beat. He pressed her against him, hands on her hips. Nat draped an arm around his neck, letting her head fall back as they moved together.

This was a bad idea. She knew it. Knew things were building to a crescendo she wouldn't be able to stop. Knew she was so going to regret it in the morning. And at the same time, she didn't care. Eric's body moving against hers, his eyes burning into hers, his hands holding her close…he was all that mattered. She didn't want anything else at that moment. Except maybe a few less layers of clothing.

Nat had been the prude in the corner looking down on the people making out on the dance floor. She sent out a mental apology to anyone she'd mentally judged over the years. Because, oh my God, she wanted nothing more than to ram her tongue down Eric's throat, and she really didn't give a flying fuck who was watching.

Eric apparently had the same idea and Nat nearly sobbed in relief when he wrapped both his arms around her waist and pressed her closer. He fisted his hand in her hair and dragged her mouth to his. Their lips met, tongues tangling, devouring each other. There was nothing gentle or sweet about it. No slow build up. They were both too amped up for that.

Eric pushed her away and Nat gasped, her eyes flying open. He smiled at her, his slightly swollen lips stretching in a sexy grin that made her weak at the knees. He spun her around and then pulled her in so her back was cradled against his chest. His arm clamped around her waist, keeping her firmly pressed to him. They swayed to the beat of the music, Eric's lips skimming up the slope of her shoulder to the sensitive spot at the base of her neck. His teeth grazed her skin and she jerked, her arm lifting to wrap around the back of his neck, keeping his mouth fixed firmly against the pulse throbbing in her throat. He broke away only long enough to move back to her lips, capturing her mouth and stealing her breath.

She twisted in his arms so she could fully face him, nipping at his bottom lip as she pulled slightly away, breaking contact. Eric's hands clamped around her waist, keeping her molded to him. A slow smile spread across Nat's lips and she let her head fall back. She wrapped a leg around his hip, letting him support her weight as her upper body arched backward, still swaying in time with him.

He brought her slowly back up, a heat burning in his eyes that she knew was echoed in her own. Bad idea as it may be, there was no turning back now. They were seconds from ripping each other's clothes off, right there on the dance floor. Nat pushed any other thought out of her head. She'd never wanted anything so badly in her whole life as she wanted him in that moment. And for once she was going to do what she wanted and be happy, and everything else could be damned.

Nat brought her lips up to Eric's ear. "Let's get out of here," she breathed, nipping his earlobe.

Eric pulled back far enough that he could look her full in the face. "You sure?"

She knew he wanted to. With his body glued to hers, he couldn't have hidden it if he tried. And she appreciated him making sure she was making a rational decision. But she was also impatient with it. There was no point denying what was between them and the only thing she wanted to do was get out of the club and go somewhere she could rip that shirt off him and get her hands on every delicious inch of his body.

She answered him by grabbing his hand and pulling him off the floor. They stopped by their table long enough for Eric to nod good-bye to Jared and grab his jacket, which he draped strategically over his arm. Nat gave Gina a little wave, ignoring her friend's shocked and amused expression, and let Eric tow her out the door.

The walk home was a blur of hands and lips and a vague sense of embarrassment whenever someone had to clear their throats to get around them on the sidewalk. Nat nearly sobbed in relief once they reached Eric's brownstone. They jogged up the stairs to the front door and Eric pulled her against him, claiming her lips again while he fumbled for the keys in his pocket. Nat vaguely realized there were still people wandering about the streets, but nothing much registered on her radar but Eric.

He dropped the keys on the stoop but neither took much notice. Eric pushed her up against his front door, his hands tangling in her hair as he angled her mouth to fit to his. She yanked his T-shirt out of his jeans, desperate to get her hands on his bare chest. He pulled the shoulder of her dress to the side, kissing across her collarbone. One thumb grazed across a nipple and Nat gasped and arched into him. He cupped her breast, bringing his mouth back to hers.

Someone coughed. Eric and Nat glanced up, disoriented, and froze when they met the shocked gaze of someone's little old night-owl grandma, apparently setting out to walk her dog. Eric nodded at her, his hand still entangled in Nat's dress, his body pressed to hers. Moving, however, would definitely be worse, seeing as how it would give the poor old woman an eyeful of the rock solid length currently straining the seams in Eric's pants.

"Good evening, Mrs. Jankowski. Going for a walk?" he asked.

Nat smiled and felt around on the ground for the keys with her foot.

Mrs. Jankowski nodded, her mouth hanging slightly open. "Just taking Peanut out."

"Got them," Nat whispered, kicking her foot out of her stiletto long enough to snake the keys with her toes. She brought her foot up behind her, grabbed the keys and shoved them into Eric's hands.

"Ah. Lovely night for it," he said, jamming his key into the lock. Nat sagged against him in relief when she heard the lock click.

"We're just on our way in. Have a good night then." Eric opened the door and they stumbled inside and slammed it, shutting out the sight of his thoroughly shocked and mildly amused neighbor.

The moment the door closed, Eric and Natalie burst out laughing.

"Oh my God, your poor neighbor."

"Yeah, I'm going to have to move for sure."

They laughed again. The movement brought Eric and his poor pants back into contact with the sensitive skin of Nat's bare thighs and her laughter choked off in a gasp. Eric's eyes locked with hers and their smiles faded.

Then his lips were on hers again, his hands roaming over every inch he could touch. Eric spun Nat into the hallway and up a flight of stairs before she could catch her breath.

They hit the second floor and she was up against the wall again. But this time they were alone. No one was going to interrupt them. Nat grabbed Eric's shirt and tugged it over his head, exposing his muscled chest. She lightly raked her nails down his chest and over his rock-hard abs, not hard enough to even redden his skin, just enough to make him shudder and groan against her mouth.

He backed up, pulling her with him through the apartment. Nat didn't even register where they were, didn't notice anything other than Eric. She kept her mouth fused with his and kicked off her shoes. Seconds later, his hit the floor with two solid thumps. He pushed her dress off her shoulders, leaving her in nothing but her bra and lacy black underwear. Eric stopped, his gaze raking her over from head to toe.

"My God. You are so beautiful."

Heat rushed to Nat's cheeks and she reached for him, pulling his head down so she could kiss him. His large warm hands encircled her waist and Nat sighed against his lips. She felt tiny and fragile and at the same time more powerful and safe than she'd ever felt before. Eric's hands trembled slightly against her skin and she smiled, loving that he was just as affected as she. The intensity building in her escalated until her whole body tingled with it. She craved Eric, wanted his touch, wanted him inside her.

She fumbled with the zipper of Eric's pants and he reached down to help. They'd reached his bedroom and he groped for the light switch. When the light blared on, Nat broke away from Eric just long enough to glance around the room. The sight of the king-sized bed, sheets still tussled from the night before, had her heart lurching into her throat. A hint of anxiety crept through her, cooling the heat of desire burning through her veins.

Then Eric's pants hit the floor and he was on his knees in front of her, his hand skimming up the back of her legs. His lips and tongue trailed up, nibbling at the soft skin of her inner thighs until he reached her overheated core. He sucked at her through the thin lace panties, his teeth lightly scraping over her until she thought her legs would give out. She sucked in a ragged breath of air, clutching at his head and shoulders.

Eric surged to his feet, scooping her up in his arms and carrying her to the bed in just a few steps. Her underwear joined his on the floor, the mattress sinking under his weight as he knelt over her. He settled between her legs, kissing his way up her body. Nat couldn't think straight anymore. Couldn't think of anything but the sensations Eric was causing. She reached for him. Pulled him to her. Groaned when his weight settled on her, the heat of his skin burning through her.

"Wait," she said, her voice coming out in a breathy whisper she barely recognized. "Do you...we need..." She couldn't get the thought out but Eric was already on it.

"Yeah, hang on, I've got..." His weight left her for a brief moment while he fumbled at the nightstand's drawer. The lamp sitting on the table crashed to the floor.

"Shit!"

Nat laughed but the movement pushed Eric's thigh against the juncture of her legs and she sucked in a strangled breath. "Eric," she said, reaching for him, "please. I need..." He pushed his leg against her again.

"I know, Cupcake."

He grabbed the box, spilling foil packets all over the bed.

"Think we'll need that many?" Nat asked with a breathy laugh.

"I like to be optimistic," he said, grabbing a packet and ripping it open.

"Good to know."

He rocked his thigh against her again while he rolled the condom on, and she gasped, rubbing against him.

His fingers slipped inside her, teasing, testing. Nat cried out, her hips lifting, straining toward him. He didn't make her wait. He guided himself inside, thrusting to the hilt in one motion. Eric held still for a second, leaning down to kiss her, letting her get used to the feel of him.

Nat was on fire. Every cell in her body throbbed with her pounding heart, every nerve ending pulsing as Eric retreated and plunged, his mouth and hands building pleasure upon pleasure until she burned with it. She wasn't going to be able to hold out for long. A few more strokes and her world exploded. She gasped his name, clinging to him as wave after wave rippled through her. His tempo increased and a few moments later he joined her, his body going rigid as he found his release.

Eric collapsed against her, rolling to the side so he wouldn't crush her. He brushed her hair out of her face, pulling her to him and tucking her against his body. He kissed her cheek, her temple, then her lips, lingering gently while their heart rates returned to normal.

• • •

Nat rolled on her side and Eric quickly cleaned up and then pulled her into him, spooning her against him so she could curl into his warmth.

"Next time," he said, turning her face so he could kiss her again, "we'll take our time."

Nat laughed, her voice low and deep, utterly spent. "Next time? Pretty confident, are you?"

"At the moment, very." Hell, he had so much adrenaline and testosterone flowing through him he was pretty sure he could jump out the window and fly. A night of marathon sex would be a piece of cake. A very delicious piece of scrumptious Cupcake. He leaned down to nuzzle her neck, pressing small, lingering kisses up the slender column and across her jawline.

"Already?" Nat murmured, her voice hitching on the last

syllable. "Are you sure you can do it again so soon?"

"Most definitely. And this time, it'll be even better."

"I don't think that's possible."

"Don't underestimate me. I'm pretty spectacular, you know."

"*Hmm*," Nat said, wiggling a little. "You don't say."

Eric sucked in his breath as her ass rubbed against him. "Feeling playful, are we?"

Nat rolled onto her stomach, looking back over her shoulder at him with the sexiest smile he'd ever seen in his life. It was all he could do not to jump on her like some savage beast and plunge into her right there and then. He'd been teasing, but to his surprise he was already completely hard and ready for her again. God, he'd never get enough of her. One taste and he was ready to follow her around like a faithful puppy for the rest of their lives.

She cocked a finger at him, biting the side of her lip, and Eric's brain short-circuited. He leaned over to run his hands down the smooth skin of her back. His lips and tongue followed, trailing their way down her spine. Her back bowed, pushing against his lips as he nibbled at the sensitive skin. He massaged the flesh of her ass, kissing the little hollow at the base of her spine. Nat moaned and Eric closed his eyes, breathing deeply in his struggle for control. He was about to lose it without even entering her. And that would be a fucking waste of epic proportions. He lay beside her and pulled her leg up over his hip. She immediately rocked against him.

He grabbed her hips, keeping her steady. He'd meant it. This time they were going slow. He was going to make it last as long as he could, until she was screaming his name, begging for release. Nat was already whimpering, her breaths coming in short, sharp pants that mingled with gasps whenever his fingers trailed across her skin. Her skin was flushed, and the sight of her straining for him made him throb to the point of pain.

Eric grabbed another condom, let her watch as he rolled it on inch by inch. Then he grasped her hips and guided himself into her as slowly as he could. He stopped and retreated an inch and Nat cried out. She tried to push against him, bring him farther inside, but he held her hips steady. He teased her. Penetrating an inch or two only to retreat. Again, and once more, until Nat's body was quivering in his grasp.

"Eric," she gasped.

He jerked against her, his name on her lips nearly undoing him. He'd meant to draw it out even longer, but he couldn't wait anymore. He rolled Nat to her back, keeping her leg wrapped firmly around his waist, and thrust hard, filling her to the core. Nat cried out, her breath ragged. He reached one hand between them to play with her engorged nipple, rolling it between his fingers as he thrust into her. His other hand grabbed her hips for support as he began to plunge into her, harder and faster. She moaned his name, rocking into him, meeting him thrust for thrust, both of them crying out.

She arched into him as she came and he collapsed on top of her, their breath mingling as they panted in spent ecstasy together. He rolled off her, gently turning her until she faced him. He kissed her, his hands cupping her face.

"I was wrong. You are the one who is spectacular."

She laughed and rested her head on his chest. "Don't sell yourself short. That was just…amazing."

"*Hmmm*. Just wait until round three."

Nat laughed again. "You're going to have to give me a few minutes."

"Not a problem. I think I need a little recoup time myself."

"I'm not sure we can best that last one."

"Oh ye of little faith," Eric said.

Before Nat could argue further, Eric set about showing her just how wrong she was. By the end of their third time, she'd lost the ability to do anything but feel the sensations Eric wrought in her body. Neither one of them spoke, but just curled up together in an exhausted heap. Eric fell asleep in the very early hours of the morning, his arms wrapped around Natalie, feeling more complete than he'd ever felt in his life.

# Chapter Six

Nat's eyes cracked open and she blinked at her surroundings, disoriented for a second. The soft sound of someone breathing next to her had her heart pounding in her throat. She slowly peeked over her shoulder at Eric snuggled up behind her. Holy hell. Part of her wanted to cuddle up against him and go back to sleep. The rest of her was flooded with such abject embarrassment she was certain she'd melt into a puddle of shame right there on the bed. His bed. That she was lying in. Naked.

She closed her eyes and rubbed her hand over her face. She had to get out of there. Before he woke up sober and she found out how he really felt about last night. She didn't think she could handle it if he opened his eyes and instantly regretted what had been the greatest sex of her life. One more reason to be grateful she wasn't tied to Steve for the rest of her life. She would have never found out just how good sex could be.

Eric sighed and burrowed farther into his pillow. Nat waited a few moments to be sure he wasn't waking up and then slipped out from under his arm as slowly and quietly as she could. The second her feet hit the floor she scurried around the room, gathering her clothes. She looked in vain for her bra and finally decided to abandon it. Her breasts would survive the quick walk home.

Nat closed her eyes again, dreading the walk of shame, as they always called it in the movies. She'd never had a one-night stand in her life. Not that Eric was a one-night stand. No, he was just someone she'd have to see at work every day for the foreseeable future. She threw her clothes on, doing her best to straighten her hair and clean up any makeup smudges. A rustling of sheets from the bedroom had her bolting down the stairs. She paused briefly to stare openmouthed at Eric's home. Damn. Gelato must do well for himself.

The faint sound of "Mamma Mia" coming from the bedroom had her moving. She briefly considered leaving a note but had no freaking clue what she'd say.

*Hi. Thanks for the screw. See you at work. Buh-bye.*

Only…it had been so much more than that. To her at least. But probably not to him. They didn't even know each other. And she wasn't the type of girl guys stuck around for. More like the type they ditched as soon as they'd taken what they wanted. She'd learned that the hard way. Nat inwardly groaned and eased out the front door, closing it as quietly as she could. She'd call him later. Once she'd had a chance to figure out what in the hell to say. Or maybe she'd just text him. That would be easier.

Right now she had bigger problems. Facing Gina. She was never going to live this down.

She'd only gotten a block when her phone buzzed. She sighed and pulled her phone out, glancing at the text coming through. Eric. Wondering where she was. Nat chewed on her lip and hurried down the street, ignoring the "I know what you did last night" glances at her disheveled club dress she got from the people she passed. She looked back at Eric's text. She had to say something.

*Sorry, supposed to meet Gina this morning. Didn't want to wake you.*

*I wouldn't have minded.*

"No, but I would have," Nat mumbled.

*Am I going to see you today?*

Nat hesitated, not sure how to respond. Did she want to see him? Yes. If she was honest with herself. Yes. She wanted very much to see him. And she couldn't deny the thrill that shot through her that he'd asked to see her. But would it be a mistake? Hell yes. An even bigger mistake than last night had been. Besides, he was probably just asking because he felt like he should. He seemed like a decent guy. He was probably just trying to be nice.

She couldn't quite bring herself to regret it. It had probably been the best night in her life. She'd never allowed herself to be so free and unrestrained. She'd never been affected by any man as much as she'd been by Eric. Her Mr. Gelato. He'd completely rocked her world. She'd never quite understood that expression until last night. Not that she had all that much experience with that sort of thing. But the other men she'd been with had never come close to completely shattering her, the way Eric did with the smallest touch, the slightest glance in her direction. Her insides were still quivering, her legs still as weak as two pillars of gelatin.

But it was never a good idea to mix business and pleasure. Right? Wasn't that also a saying? So it must be true. Otherwise, it wouldn't be a saying. She should care about all that. Right? But she really just wanted to see him again.

*Sure :)*

*Excellent—when and where?*

Nat tried to keep a smile from breaking out but couldn't quite manage it. Where would be a good spot to meet? They could go to one of her favorite spots, but it was a little on the romantic side, cozy and secluded. But hell, they *had* just spent the night together. A little romance really wasn't out of the question.

*There's this romantic little bistro not too far from my building. We could meet there…one o'clock?*

Nat waited for a response. Five minutes had never felt so long. She should have picked someplace else. He was probably completely freaking out over the "romantic" bit. Maybe he thought *she* thought they were in a relationship now or something. Or maybe he was just after a quick repeat of last night and here she was getting all lovey-dovey. She definitely shouldn't have said romantic. He was probably freaking out…

*Shit. Sorry, Nat. I just realized what day it was. I've got a lunch date I have to go to.*

But she couldn't stop a twinge of jealousy from slapping at her. She was being ridiculous. For all she knew it was with some eighty-year-old blue-haired lady with false teeth and cataracts. That thought made her feel marginally better. Fine. Whatever. Blow it off and play it cool. Nat blew a breath out, fluttering her bangs out of her face, and texted Eric back.

*No problem. Crazy busy today, anyway. Huge cupcake order to fill for a party.*

*I'm really sorry. I'm meeting with my parents. Business talk. I'd rather take a nice, long lunch with you.*

Nat smiled, despite herself. Well, she couldn't really blame him. Business and parents—definitely impossible to get out of.

*Go be a good little financial consultant. I'll see you next Monday.*

*That's an awfully long time from now.*

Nat grinned, trying and failing to tamp down the happiness flooding through her. It had been one day and already her emotions were playing yo-yo. Lovely.

*It's only a few days. Party time is over, Gelato. Go to work.*

What the hell was she doing? She was flirting with him.

*Fine. But I'll text you later tonight.*

*If you must.*

*I must. Have a good day, Cupcake.*

Nat tucked her phone away, no longer caring that she was walking down the street in last night's dress, grinning like a fool.

Her smile faded the second she walked into her apartment and came face to face with Gina.

"Well, I guess I don't have to ask how last night went," Gina said, smirking.

Nat dropped her stuff on the floor and flopped onto the

couch with a groan. "I'm so screwed."

Gina snorted. "I bet you are."

Nat chucked a pillow at her. "That's not what I meant!"

"Oh, what, so you're telling me you didn't get laid last night?"

Nat just buried her face back in the couch and Gina laughed. "That's what I thought."

"What am I going to do?"

"What do you mean?"

"What do you mean, what do I mean? I just slept with the guy I'm supposed to be working for, or with, or whatever."

"It's not like the guy is your boss, Nat."

"I know, but still."

Gina shrugged. "So you had one night of fun. It doesn't have to be a big deal unless you make it one. As long as it doesn't happen again, you're fine."

"What do you mean?"

"This is the guy that owns the bakery you are going to be using. The guy that wants the parking spot that belongs to you. Things might be great now, but what happens when it's not so great? Are you going to lose the kitchen time? Will he be a pain over the whole garage situation? Last night was one thing. You guys had a little too much to drink maybe, got a little carried away, had a mutually fun night. End of story."

"He wanted to see me today."

Gina's eyes narrowed.

"Don't worry, I'm not going to," Nat said. Gina's eyes narrowed further. "He's got a business lunch with his parents."

"All right then. I mean, don't get me wrong, I'm glad you got a little somethin' last night. About damn time, if you ask me. And it was special circumstances. If he tries to make it more…well, how do you know he's not just doing it to get on your good side?"

Nat hugged a cushion to her chest. Gina was right. It hurt

more than Nat liked to admit, but it was true.

"Come on, Natty Bear. Go get cleaned up. We've got a shit-ton of cupcakes to bake."

• • •

"Oh come on, dude. You've got to give me more details than that."

Eric's eyes narrowed, his patience with Jared dwindling quickly. Not that he'd ever been big on kissing and telling, but for some reason his friend wanting to hear details about Natalie really rubbed him the wrong way.

"There's nothing to tell," he insisted.

"Right. You sure about that?" Jared was staring at something near the ceiling.

Eric glared at Jared's smug tone but followed his gaze, his heart rate kicking up a notch when he saw Nat's lacy black bra hanging from the light fixture above the dining table. How the hell had that gotten up there? He climbed on a chair and yanked it down, shoving it in his pocket.

"Not a word," he warned Jared.

"Wouldn't dream of it."

Eric glared at him again, but while Jared's amusement remained, he didn't say anything else.

"So when are you going to see her again?"

"Next Monday."

Jared's eyes widened a little in surprise. "Monday, huh? So I guess last night didn't go so well, after all." Jared held up his hands and ducked as the remote went whizzing by his head. "I'm just saying…she snuck out of here before you woke up and now she doesn't want to see you until you start working together? Seems a little suspicious doesn't it?"

"She didn't want to wake me up, probably thought I'd be hungover. And we were going to make plans, but I've got to meet my parents."

Eric did have a nice little headache forming, but the cause of that was more Jared-related than booze-related.

"Sure. Or maybe she just wanted to make sure she was on your good side and thought a little something on the side might make it a little easier to get what she wants."

Eric frowned. "And what would that be?"

"Seriously? She just inherited a garage. Next to a bakery. And she, unlike you, actually knows what to do with one of those."

"So what, you don't think she'll be content to just show me how to run it and then walk away?"

Jared shrugged. "I'm not saying she pimped herself out for a share in the bakery or anything. But it wouldn't hurt to be careful."

Eric's frown deepened, the residual endorphins from last night beginning to dissipate.

Eric headed for his room. "I'm going to take a shower."

He closed his door before Jared could offer up any other helpful suggestions. He wished he could totally blow off Jared's concerns, but the thought had dug its claws in his brain. He kicked the shower on, his mind running over every moment of the previous night. And he remembered every single one in vivid detail. In fact, if he didn't stop remembering he was going to need to blast the cold water. No. Last night wasn't about using him or getting something from him. It was so much more than that. Even if she wasn't ready to admit it yet.

But that didn't mean he wouldn't be careful. She definitely had her guard up, and until he figured out how to get past it, it wouldn't hurt to play it safe. For now. In the meantime, he had bigger problems. His parents would be waiting for him at their favorite restaurant for their monthly lunch date. Eric was pretty sure his mother really did just want to spend time with him, but his father's motives for the monthly check-ins weren't nearly as paternal. They felt more like human resources reviews. The CEO keeping tabs on the little employees, making sure everyone was doing the job assigned to them.

Eric ignored the slight twinge of guilt at that thought. He knew his dad meant well. And he owed his parents a lot. They'd sent him to the best schools, made sure he always had the best opportunities. They'd footed all the bills and done what they could to set him up for a great life. Resenting them for that triggered a therapy-worthy guilt trip. He knew they just wanted the best for him. But the only reason he had been allowed the few choices he'd made on his own was because those choices had been ones he'd known his family would approve. What would happen when they didn't approve?

He was about to find out. Somehow, he didn't think running a bakery was on his father's list of sanctioned occupations.

An hour later, he sat looking back and forth between his parents as they digested the news he'd just shared. His mother frowned slightly and glanced worriedly at her husband. Jerry Schneider wiped his mouth with his linen napkin and laid it calmly beside his plate before leaning back in his chair and pinning his son with his most penetrating gaze. The one that had kept Eric in line since he was in diapers.

"Let me make sure I understand this correctly."

Eric took a deep breath as unobtrusively as possible. He'd never openly defied his father before. But it might have been too much to hope that his dad would just shake his hand and give him his blessing.

"You're walking away from a promising career at our investment firm in order to open a...bakery?"

"No, I'm not walking away from anything. Just yet. I've got some vacation time saved up. I'll still have my job to fall back on if the bakery doesn't work out."

"Son, you know nothing about running any sort of business, let alone a bakery."

"That's not true. I do have an MBA, so I know the basics. And I'm not doing it alone."

"You've taken on a partner?"

"Of a sort."

His father's frown deepened, concern etched across his face. "Explain."

"Aunt Franny's will left the bakery to me, but left the garage to someone else."

"What? What nonsense. What are you talking about?"

"She left the garage to her tenant, a woman named Natalie Moran. Natalie is a baker. She owns a mobile cupcakery. She's agreed to help me get the bakery up and running."

"A mobile cupcakery? You mean she's one of those food truck people that are parked over by the train station?" His father gave a short, humorless laugh. "Really son, I thought we'd raised you to be smarter than this. So what, she's just decided to help you out of the goodness of her heart? Please tell me you aren't that naive."

"No. We've worked out an arrangement to our mutual benefit."

"*Um-hmm.* Is she pretty?"

"Jerry," his mother broke in, her tone faintly chiding.

"Oh come on, Miranda. We both know our son doesn't always have the best head on his shoulders when it comes to women. How much money have his poor choices in companions cost us over the years, eh? There was the one that wanted money for that charity she was running, and the last one cost the family a million-dollar investment in her internet start-up—"

"Which is doing well enough to turn you a profit now," Eric reminded his dad, who ignored him.

"And let us not forget the gag money we had to pay to

that reporter to keep your name out of the paper when that waitress you were so sure was "the one" got arrested for drug possession."

Eric tried not to squirm. No one liked being reminded of their dumb mistakes. "That was a long time ago, Dad."

"Not long enough."

Eric took a deep breath, quickly losing his rein on his temper. Yes, he'd made some bad choices, believing the lies women told him who wanted nothing more than what he had in his bank account. But this was different. He hoped.

"There must be something in this for this food truck girl. What does she want? A partnership in the bakery? More money when you buy her out? She figures if she's nice, maybe gives you what you want, you'll pay up at the end?"

"Why do you always believe the worst of people? Natalie isn't like that."

"Oh really? And how do you know? How long have you known her?"

Eric pressed his lips together, not wanting to answer that question.

"Just as I thought," his dad said.

"We're just looking out for you, Eric. It's what parents do," his mom said.

He sighed, his anger fading a bit. "I know, Mom. But this is strictly a business arrangement," Eric insisted, pushing away images of Nat's long, silken limbs entwined around his.

"Right," his dad said. "So you're going to quit a lucrative career to what? Become a *baker*? What happened to you joining my firm? Creating Schneider and Son? I thought that was the plan."

Well, that was a guilt-laden sucker punch to the gut. His dad had been talking about Schneider and Son since Eric was a kid. Sadly, it wasn't what Eric wanted to do. But how do you tell the man who's worked his whole life to build a business that he could leave to you, that you don't want it?

A million possibilities burned on Eric's tongue but he didn't give voice to any of them. Not yet. "I told you, I'm not quitting my job. I've got enough time saved up to take a few months' leave from the firm. And I'm not saying this will be long-term. I'd like to get it up and running and see how it goes from there. Aunt Franny's bakery was very successful when it was open. The basic elements are all still in place. There's no reason it can't be successful again. Would owning another successful business really be such a bad idea?"

His father's mouth finally quirked into a partial smile. "Owning it is one thing. Running it is something entirely different, and you know it."

"Well," Eric continued, "if it doesn't fly, the building is still a valuable piece of real estate, and would be more so with an operating business on the premises. It's worth a shot."

His dad chewed that over for a minute. "At the very least, we should have John look into contesting the will. It's obvious my sister was not quite in a sound state of mind to split up a property to some girl off the streets no one has even heard of. How do we know that this woman didn't coerce the property out of Fran?"

"I know Natalie. She would never do something like that."

"Even so, it's for your own protection—"

"Fine, have your lawyer look into it. But I'm sure he'll find everything is as it should be."

"It never hurts to explore all your options."

Eric kept his mouth shut, hoping that would be an end to it. He held his breath while his dad stared him down. Finally, his father gave a sharp nod. Eric allowed himself to relax a bit.

"Fine. If you want to waste your vacation time playing baker with some food truck girl, that's your decision. But for once in your life, will you take my advice and keep your eyes open? It's an odd situation, to say the least. And until we know for sure what's going on, it'd be best to err on the side of caution and not sink too much into the place. Or to your… *business partner*."

Anger flashed through Eric at his father's insinuation but he kept his mouth shut. Arguing about Nat would just make his father more certain there was something going on and he knew his dad was just trying to protect him. There was no point getting into the issue with him when Eric didn't know himself what was between them. Instead, he nodded. "I'll keep my eyes open," he said.

"Good. If everything is on the up-and-up, we'll see about chipping in whatever you need to get things started."

"That would be great, Dad, thanks."

His dad nodded and got back to his meal. Eric released a pent-up breath and took a deep drink of his wine. He hoped whatever their lawyer dug up would put their minds at ease, so they'd be willing to back him, if necessary. Which it probably would. Especially since he would eventually need to buy Nat out and waiting for the bakery to make enough of a profit to do that would take a lot more time than he'd like. But that wasn't something he needed to worry about just yet.

For now, he was thankful he'd gotten off so easy and he wasn't going to stir the pot any more than necessary.

# Chapter Seven

Nat closed her eyes and tried to count to ten, her fingers gripping the clipboard she held in an effort not to chuck the thing at Eric's head. All thoughts of their night together and any worries over awkwardness or her vague answers to his repeated texts over the past week had evaporated within five minutes of his arrival at the bakery. They didn't agree on anything. Literally, *nothing*. From paint swatches to the menu to baking equipment to the basic layout of the store. Nothing. And Nat had about reached her limit. If he wasn't going to take her advice, why was she even here?

"Look," she said, "I know this is your bakery, so you have final say. But if you are going to do something, you might as well do it right. You asked for my help because I knew what I was doing, so why do you question *everything* that I say?"

Exhaustion pulled at her. She'd already been up for hours, getting the cupcakes for the truck ready to go and helping Gina stock up for the day before seeing her off. Being tired certainly didn't help her mood.

Eric's voice penetrated the tiny cocoon of calm she'd

almost created for herself before she hit seven on her countdown.

"I don't question *everything*. But I don't see what's wrong with putting baklava on the menu. It's a popular dessert."

Nat took a deep breath and opened her eyes. Eric frowned, his frustration as apparent as hers. He leaned against the counter in the kitchen, bulging arms folded across his chest in what would normally be a delicious display of manly yumminess. But right now, his good looks weren't buying him any brownie points.

"Baklava would be great. For a Greek bakery. Not for an Italian bakery. It's all about branding. If you want to name the bakery Tuscan Treats and serve Italian pastries, you need to focus on Italian pastries. You can't just slap a Greek dish on the menu because it's popular. Your customers need to know what they'll be getting when they come here."

"Isn't that what the menu is for?"

Nat sighed, rubbing a hand over the dull ache that was beginning to form at her temples. "Yes, but a customer looking for baklava isn't going to see Tuscan Treats in the phone book and think 'Ooo, Greek desserts.' You are trying to entice people who want Italian pastries. It'd be like going to a mattress store and buying a dining room table. Just because they're both pieces of furniture doesn't mean they belong in the same store."

"Who uses a phone book anymore?"

"Eric!"

He threw his hands up and edged a little farther away from her, his lips twitching. If he smiled, he was going to get a whisk shoved where the sun didn't shine.

"That's not my point, and you know it."

"Fine, I get it. No baklava."

Nat sighed. Finally, a decision on something. She glanced back at the list on her clipboard.

"So, I guess calling the bakery Schneider's Tuscan Treats would be out of the question, too?" Eric asked, grinning at her.

Nat's eyes narrowed. "Not unless you want people wandering in looking for fresh baked strudel and a chef in lederhosen."

"Hey, I would rock a pair of lederhosen. I totally have the legs for it." He hiked one pant leg up and shoved the exposed limb in her direction.

Nat tried to keep the laugh in but it came out in a sort of strangled snort. Eric's eyes widened and Nat turned around, her cheeks flaming. "Put that leg away or I'll make you put a hair net on it."

Eric laughed. "I'm not that hairy." He looked at the limb in question, squinted at the mass of curly blond hair covering it and lowered his pant leg. "Okay, fine. I'm all covered up and decent. What's next on the list, Boss Lady?"

Nat ran her pen down the checklist. She wasn't sure why she'd bothered to alphabetize it. Getting Eric to stick to any sort of organization was futile. "You still have to make a final decision on decor, get someone in here to check all this equipment, since you insist on using it, then—"

"Why can't we use it? I don't see the point in buying new equipment when we have a kitchen full of it already."

"Because, like I've already said, this stuff is fifty years old, at least. You don't even know if it works or if it's up to code, and I seriously doubt it is. Repairing and restoring it will probably cost a lot more than just replacing it."

"Maybe, but if it does work and is up to code, I'd like to keep it. It adds to the ambiance of the place."

"No one will even see it."

"You can see a hint of it from the outside counter." Eric ran a hand over the ancient stove. "They don't make them like this anymore. Besides, it was my aunt's. I'd like to keep some part of her here."

That was surprisingly sentimental. Not what Nat had expected from him. It was…sweet. "All right, it's your kitchen, but it still needs to be checked out, so I'll make a note to call someone to come look at everything."

Eric nodded. "Fine. As for the decor, we already discussed that. I want the old plaster look, vines, plantation shutters. Make it look like an old villa."

He waited, probably expecting an argument, but he relaxed a bit when Nat kept her mouth shut. She'd already voiced her opinion that making it look like every other Italian restaurant/bakery/shop in the country was a bit cliché, so she wasn't going to try and change his mind again. It probably wouldn't be fatal. And she could hopefully slip in a few modern touches that would make the place look like an Italian villa without making it look like a mini Olive Garden. The seating though…

"The decor is fine, but as for the tables — "

"I don't see what your objection is to outside seating."

"I have no objection," she said, trying to keep her tone even and patient. "My objection is to *only* having outdoor seating. This is New Jersey. It gets cold in the winter. Your customers might enjoy someplace warm to sit and enjoy their dessert."

"Yes, but the front area is fairly small. If the place is busy, which I hope it will be, there won't be much room for customers to come in and browse. We'll definitely need some tables on the sidewalk out front. And the little side alley is perfect for garden seating if we get a permit. You know, once we clean it up and get some plants out there."

"Yes," she said, her tone getting a little less patient, "but if there is nowhere to sit down inside once they've purchased something, they might not bother purchasing anything at all. Not everyone will be getting something to go. Some might want to eat their purchase here. Inside."

"Yes…" His tone matched hers. "But I don't see how we'll fit in the new counters we talked about and still have booths for seating."

Nat bit her tongue. His concern wasn't entirely unfounded. But people had to have somewhere to sit. "Okay. So, why don't we cut out the booths and instead do some small tables? The pretty wrought iron bistro sets that only sit two or three people. That would discourage large groups from hanging out all day but would still give people some seating options for when the weather is bad."

Eric paused for a second and then nodded. "All right, we can at least draw up the plans and see what it'll look like."

"Good." Nat smiled and jotted some notes on her growing list of things to do.

"Why don't we take a break for a little bit. Go grab some lunch," Eric said.

The mention of food seemed to remind Nat's stomach that she hadn't fed it anything since six that morning. The small cramp would give way to a full-on growl soon, but she hated to stop now that they were actually making progress. She frowned and checked her watch. "It's only eleven thirty."

Eric shrugged. "We've earned it. Come on. We've gotta eat."

Her stomach agreed, erupting in a growl that had Eric's eyebrows disappearing into his hairline. Nat gave in to a rueful grin. She couldn't argue with him *and* her rumbling belly. She put down her clipboard. "All right. A short break. Where to?"

Twenty minutes later, she was seated in the Greek restaurant down the street, a steaming plate of chicken souvlaki with lemon rice and potatoes in front of her. Along with a platter of sticky sweet baklava. Eric winked at her and popped a piece in his mouth.

"Ah," he sighed. "Sweet nectar of the gods."

Nat laughed and picked up her fork. "Do you always eat dessert first?"

"Why wait for the good stuff?" he asked, taking a bite of another piece and licking a few honey-encrusted crumbs from his lips.

Nat froze, watching the trail his tongue took across his full lower lip. Her fork hovered in the air near her mouth, her breath in sudden short supply. When he put his finger in his mouth and sucked the last bit of honey off it, she forgot to breathe altogether.

Eric stilled, watching her watch him. A slow smile spread over his lips and he leaned over, holding out the pastry. "You want a bite?"

Nat sat back, the blood rushing to her cheeks again. She'd been staring at him like a cat drooling over a bowl of cream. A delicious, infinitely lickable bowl of cream. "No, thanks," she mumbled, shoving a piece of chicken in her mouth.

Eric shrugged. "Don't know what you're missing."

Actually, she did. That was the problem. Just thinking of the night they'd spent together had certain body parts quivering in remembered ecstasy, and warmth pooled in her belly. She desperately ached for more.

He finished the baklava and then turned to the lamb gyro on his plate.

"So, what else do we need to accomplish today?" he asked.

Nat relaxed, grateful for the return to safe conversation. She didn't know what her deal was with this guy. He got under her skin like no one else. Their night, far from scratching the itch, had made every cell in her body crave more of him. How could she be so turned on by someone who drove her absolutely insane? The man knew nothing about baking, let alone running a bakery, and having to teach someone how to do something she'd dreamed of doing her whole life was tough to take. It seemed like her brain was constantly debating between shoving him off a cliff or sticking her tongue down his throat. He unnerved her, to say the least.

But he also made the blood pulse in her veins like liquid fire. She was going to get seasick from the roller coaster her emotions were on if she didn't get her head back in the game and keep her hormones in the locker room where they belonged.

"Not much," she answered him. "We've got enough to get going, for sure. I'll call some people this afternoon about coming to look at the equipment in the kitchen. I think that's the most important thing for right now. Can't very well have a bakery if you can't bake anything. And then, the next big project is cleaning the place up and getting it redecorated. I'll draw up some plans for possible layouts for the space. We can visit some places I know of where we can get some good deals on furniture. The display cases already there might work fine if we refurbish them a bit."

She scooped a forkful of rice into her mouth, but only about half of the stuff made it inside. The rest took a nosedive off her silverware and trickled into her bra. She sighed and lowered her fork. "Every time," she muttered, peeking into the dark recesses of her shirt.

Eric laughed. "Need a little help with that?"

Nat narrowed her eyes at him but couldn't stop a sheepish grin from breaking out. She wiped her mouth with her napkin. "No, thank you."

"Mamma Mia" rang out from Eric's phone. Holy crap, that woman called a lot. Nat stood. Might as well give him some mommy time and go clean herself up.

"Excuse me," she said as Eric answered the phone. She stood and made her way to the bathroom, trying to ignore the chuckle that followed her. She went into the first stall and started digging rice out of her bra. She'd always been blessed with ample cleavage and, if she were honest, had enjoyed the benefits of a nice full C cup. Having food fall down her shirt on an almost daily basis wasn't one of the perks. Unless she was wearing something with a tight neck, any bits of food that might not make it all the way to her mouth (something that happened with distressing frequency) tended to slip right into the nice cavern created by her chest.

Once she'd vacated the food from her lingerie, she went to the sink and washed the traces of oily lemon seasoning from her hands. She glanced in the mirror.

"You have got to chill," she told herself. She needed to finish helping Eric with his bakery so she could get away from him and get back to her regular life.

Though, with her new parking spot attached to his bakery and part of her payment for helping him being the use of his kitchen, she wouldn't be able to escape him totally. But anything was better than this roller coaster. And it was only Day One.

"You're in such deep shit," she said to her reflection.

She took a deep breath and went back out to face the object of her obsession.

When she got back to the table, Eric was standing there waiting for her. Their food was boxed, bagged, and paid for.

"Are we leaving?" she asked.

"I'm sorry. A friend is flying in and my mother wants me to play taxi driver."

"Don't they have actual taxi drivers for that sort of thing?"

Eric's lips pulled into a wry grin. "Yes. But Courtney is a family friend and my mom wants me to play nice. We can finish up whatever is next on your list tomorrow. I promise."

"Courtney, huh?"

Eric's grin widened. "She's just a friend. And the daughter of one of my father's investors. So…"

"So, you have to play nice."

"Exactly."

"All right, go play chauffeur. But I'm holding you to your promise, Gelato. We've got a lot of work to do."

"Wouldn't miss it for the world, Cupcake."

# Chapter Eight

One week and six furniture stores later, Eric was ready to buy anything Natalie showed him, just to end the torture. Well, almost anything. The newest "store" was actually an old warehouse that had been converted into an antique store of sorts. Nat stood next to some ridiculously flimsy arts and crafts project with a hopeful look.

Eric stared down at the table with a frown. "This is the table you're suggesting?"

"Yes. Why, what's wrong with it?"

"Are you kidding me? It's so girly. Isn't there something a little more manly we can choose?"

"Sure. I suppose we could drag in some ratty old pool table for your customers to eat on. Is that what you had in mind?"

"No," he said, his voice tight with irritation. She'd dragged him to more furniture stores than any man should have to visit and they still hadn't found anything they could agree on. Her reasoning made sense and definitely showed she knew what she was doing, so it was hard to argue with her. But now, she wanted him to buy a flimsy little table that looked like the ratty lace things his grandmother used to put under her potted plants. And the two chairs that came with it didn't look like they'd fit a toddler's ass, let alone a full-grown human's. He jammed his fingers through his hair and concentrated on taking a few deep breaths.

"No," he said again. "But I'm sure we could find something that doesn't look like it belongs in a dollhouse."

Nat rubbed her forehead but not before he caught a distinct eye roll aimed in his direction.

"They aren't that small," she said. "And they are perfect for the atmosphere you are going for. It is exactly something you would find on the terrace of a Tuscan villa. They're beautiful and they are small, so they won't take up much space. Which means we'll be able to put in enough to have adequate seating without cluttering up the shop. I thought that's what you wanted."

"Yeah, that sounds great. But I would like my customers to be able to fit their entire ass on their chair without having one cheek hanging off."

The corner of Nat's mouth twitched up and though she tried to keep from smiling he could see she was losing the battle.

"They aren't that bad."

He raised an eyebrow.

"You've never even sat in one before." She pointed to the chair nearest him. "Try it before you totally veto it."

He repressed a sigh and pulled out a chair just to shut her up. But when he sat down he found that it really was a lot better than he thought. Yes, it was small and made of iron, but it really wasn't all that uncomfortable and the important bits and pieces of his lower anatomy were supported well enough. The table was small but it would certainly work for a few plates and cups. Which was all that he needed.

He hated admitting she was right. She watched him with a growing smile.

"Fine," he said with a sigh. "But do we have to get them in white? It just reminds me of some garden tea party."

"Been to many of those, have you?"

He glared at her and she laughed. "Fine. Black would work just as well. We can paint them."

"Well, hallelujah. We finally agree on something."

"Oh hush. It hasn't been that bad."

He grinned but chose not to respond to that particular comment. "So. What's next?"

Nat looked down at the ever-present clipboard in her hand. "Well, we've got the tables and chairs covered now, we chose the window coverings this morning, we've got our paint samples to take back to the shop, so the only thing left is…" She paused while she ran her pen down the list. "The dishes and silverware."

He took a breath, gearing up for another argument. She'd briefly mentioned her thoughts on the whole silverware thing earlier, but then they'd gotten tangled up in a discussion over the difference between white and ecru (which he still didn't believe was actually a color) and the fork issue had been left hanging.

"Right. About the silverware…"

Nat looked up, her eyes already narrowing. Eric couldn't stop a grin from peeking out. As frustrating as these shopping trips were, it was kind of fun to rile her up. Still, if he wanted to get his way, sometime in this century, it might be better to tread lightly. He held up his hands in the universal gesture for "I come in peace" and aimed what he hoped was a charming smile at her.

"I want this to be a nice place, classy, upscale."

"And I agree about having nice plates for those who eat at the shop."

"But?"

She folded her arms over the clipboard she held to her chest. "But…plastic utensils would make your life so much easier."

Eric groaned. "Plastic is so cheap! Why do you object to actual silverware?"

"It's not that I object to silverware. It just makes more sense to use plastic. It's not a full-scale restaurant. Yes, you'll offer some seating, but it's not like you'll have waiters and busboys roaming the store. Same with the plates but at least those will look nice and can be washed quickly. But silverware will just create more work for the kitchen, and they are easier to steal, so they are nothing but money walking out the door. Besides most people won't be staying to eat, but will be taking their food to go, so it's probably a moot point, anyway."

"Moot?" he said, loving when those soft lips of hers pulled into a half smile.

"Yes, moot."

"You're killing me here, you know that, right?"

"Not my intention, I promise. A bonus, maybe, but not my intention."

Eric snorted and tried not to smile. "Fine," he said, not willing to fight with her about it anymore. "But, if we are doing plastic, can we at least get the nice kind? You know the heavy-duty stuff that has some design to it, not just the flimsy little white things?"

"Deal," she said with a smile. "And you know, they do make some pretty nice plastic plates nowadays…"

"Natalie!"

She laughed and he drank in the sight of her, loving the way her eyes flashed at him.

"All right, all right. Just a suggestion. I don't think it would hurt to keep our options open but we can check out your plates first. Where are they?"

"I've got a place in the city where we can go."

Her head jerked up, her gaze locking with his. That hadn't quite sounded the way he'd meant it, but he had no intention of correcting it.

Nat hesitated. It was fascinating watching the play of emotions run across her face. Eyes widening in surprise. Cheeks flushing, breath coming a little faster. Remembering their night together? Good. Because he couldn't get it out of his head. Her lips pulled into a slight smile. *Hmmm*. And what was that look all about?

She took a step closer. "Your place, huh? Mine would be better," she said, tapping the tip of her pen on his chest.

He held his breath. Well, that was unexpected. Did she mean it? Surely not. She hadn't shown any sign of wanting a repeat performance. She stepped even closer, the vanilla and cinnamon scent of her enveloping him. He almost leaned down, almost closed the remaining few inches between them, but Jared's unwelcome warnings pushed their way through the hormone haze in his head and Eric checked himself.

He shoved his hands into his pockets to keep from reaching out to touch her. He knew she tasted just as good as she smelled and the urge to refresh his memory was making his body harden in all the wrong places. Well, in all the right places actually, just the way wrong time.

"It might be fun going to my place," she said.

Eric froze. Seriously? He squinted at her, trying to figure out what game she was playing. Because there was no way she meant that.

"I've got another book of fabric swatches there we could look over…"

Eric laughed and stepped back, the tension dissipating a bit. He should have known better. "I meant, what store do you want to go to next?"

Nat grinned at him. "Okay, I know you have your heart

set on those china plates you were telling me about. But if you just keep an open mind, they actually have some great options here."

He shook his head, hardly believing he was caving again. "All right. Fine. Show me what they've got."

Her smile lit up her face, immediately rewarding him for the compromise. "Yay! Just let me jot some notes down real quick," she said, turning back to the damned clipboard. She added, "They've got a clearance sale going on."

Economizing wasn't something he was used to doing but until his parents came around and were willing to throw a few bucks his way, clearance sales were his new best friend.

"All right, let's go shop some sales."

"Ah, don't look so depressed. I know shopping isn't your thing, but maybe you'll get lucky."

Eric closed his eyes and inwardly groaned. She was going to be the death of him. He wished he could get lucky. He immediately mentally slapped himself for the thought but he couldn't help himself. Thoughts like that had been popping into his head at the most inopportune moments ever since he'd met her. And it had only been getting worse the more he got to know her.

Every time she bent over to clean something, chewed on the corner of that delicious mouth while she was deep in thought, and especially every time she disagreed with him, he wanted to throw her over his shoulder and march her straight back to his bed. Her face lit up with a faint glow when she was on the defense, her eyes flashed fire when she'd argue her point. She was something pretty special to look at in any circumstance but when she was angry she was damn near spectacular. And since she'd spent the majority of their time together ready to cave his skull in with that clipboard of hers, he'd been doing a lot of mental slapping lately.

He couldn't wait for the bakery to be up and running

so they could forget about the business and focus on a little fun. Though he tried to slip it in whenever he could. Bad choice of words. He tried to lighten the mood whenever possible. It wasn't as hard as he thought. Nat had a fun side to her that she couldn't quite keep repressed, though she obviously tried to bury it under a mountain of alphabetical lists and organizational charts. He didn't know why she was so determined to do nothing but work. He'd always been a firm believer in having fun while you got the job done.

But in this instance, maybe Nat was right to keep things a little more formal between them. Because he could see the fun getting out of hand. If she ever took her nose out of her paperwork. Nat stood beside him flipping through the papers on that damned clipboard and muttering to herself as she checked off boxes and jotted down notes.

"We're going to have to surgically remove that thing from your hand."

"Huh?" she asked, somehow managing to lift her face in his direction without taking her eyes from the papers in front of her.

Eric reached over and gently grasped her chin, turning her to face him. She jerked in surprise but didn't pull away enough to remove his hand from her face.

"What?" she asked, startled.

He smiled at her, waiting until she slowly smiled back before he let go of her face and answered. "Just worried about you is all."

She laughed. "Worried about me? Why?"

He shrugged. "Imminent failing eyesight? Carpal tunnel syndrome? Pinching your finger on the clipboard clippy thingy?"

One of her eyebrows raised and he grinned. "Don't get me wrong. I'm thrilled you are so organized. I'd never be able to keep everything straight. It seems like there's a million things we need to get done and believe me, I'm glad I put you in charge of making sure everything happens. But I swear if you look at that clipboard one more time I'm going to have to chuck it in the nearest trash can."

Nat laughed. "Just one more…" She made a quick note and then shoved the thing into her bag. "Better?"

Eric nodded. "Much." He held his hand out to her. "Lead the way to the dishes."

She smiled, glancing up at him through her lashes, and his heart lurched. Good God, did the woman even know how tempting she was?

He really hoped he'd get the chance to show her. And soon.

# Chapter Nine

Eric wandered with Nat up and down the aisles of the store, paying more attention to Nat as she glanced at the wares on display than he did to the plates and dinky little teacups she stopped to check out every now and then.

The emotions that flashed across her face were fascinating to watch. Amusement, in the wry little quirk of her mouth at the strange birds on one pattern. A slight frown, narrowed eyes at a gaudy floral pattern. Hazel eyes widening a bit, lips pressed together as she gave an interesting pattern a second glance. It was like reading a book. Every feeling there for him to see. Except when she looked at him. Odd that someone so open in every other aspect of her life kept things so hidden when it came to him.

"Oh!" she said. "There we go." She pointed at a large red sign that said *Clearance* and grabbed his hand, pulling him toward the display.

He was a lot more interested in the warm smoothness of her fingers entwined with his than he was with a bunch of plates nobody wanted but she let go before he had a chance to really enjoy it.

"What do you think of these?" She held up a plate with a simple band of green edging the rim.

He shrugged. "They're okay. A little boring."

"Okay. Next." She put the plate down but in her haste to move to the next selection, she didn't put it far enough on the display table. The moment she released it, it began to fall.

"Crap!" She grabbed for it and managed to fumble it twice before somehow slinging it in Eric's direction.

He lunged for it, snatching it just before it hit the ground. He released a long breath and carefully replaced the plate. "I said it was boring. That just meant I didn't want to buy it. I didn't mean to imply you should smash the poor thing out of existence."

Her face flushed bright red. "Sorry."

"My mother always used to tell me to put my hands in my pockets and look with my eyes, not with my hands. It irritated me at the time but I'm starting to think that might be good advice."

"Oh, shut up," she said, glaring at him.

He couldn't keep the smirk off his face. She was too fun to rile up.

A bubbly saleswoman who was all of five feet nothing bounded up on six-inch stilettos and aimed a huge smile at Eric. "Hey, I'm Jill. Can I help you find something?"

Eric glanced at her. "No thanks. We're just looking."

"Actually," Nat said, "is this all that's left of the clearance items or do you have anything else in back?"

The saleswoman frowned while she thought for a second. "I think this is most of the stuff. We might have a few boxes in back that haven't been put out yet. A lot of this stuff is surplus we're trying to move to make room for new stock. I can go check and see what we got back there. Is there anything in particular you're looking for?"

"Yes, do you have anything with either a leaf or vine pattern or maybe something in a terra-cotta color?"

"I'll go see what we've got." Jill aimed another overly-whitened grin at Eric. "You're so sweet helping your sister shop."

Nat's jaw dropped but before she could respond, Eric frowned at the saleswoman and reached over to Nat, wrapping an arm around her waist and pulling her close to his side.

"This gorgeous lady is my fiancée," he said.

He felt Nat start in surprise and he tightened his grip so she couldn't pull away. He didn't know why he cared that the saleswoman automatically assumed that he and Nat weren't a couple, but he did. He also didn't like the fake smile she shot at Nat. Eric pressed a quick kiss to Nat's forehead and she froze.

Okay, that might have been playing it up a bit too much. Then again, she wasn't trying to move away from him.

Jill glanced back and forth between them and Nat smiled at her with a strange lopsided grin that had Eric biting the inside of his cheek to keep from laughing.

"Oh. Well, isn't that great?" Jill said, though it was obvious she thought it was anything but great. "In that case, would you guys like to fill out our registry form? That way if you find a pattern you like we will have it on file for your guests."

"That sounds great," Eric said, his smile growing when Nat looked up at him, her eyes round with surprise. "But I'm not sure we've got time to do the whole registry thing right now. We're actually just shopping for everyday stuff today. Just wanted to pop in real quick and see if you had a pattern that we were interested in."

He could feel Nat trying to unobtrusively move away from him and he gripped her tighter, letting his hand slide farther down. He patted her hip and gave her a huge smile. She narrowed her eyes at him but she stayed put.

"All right, well I'll just go check and see what we've got in back then."

As soon as she disappeared behind the back doors, Nat pushed away from him but her playful smile belied the irritated tone she was going for. "What was that all about?"

Eric shrugged. "Just trying to have a little fun. We've been shopping all day. I'm about ready to blow my brains out." He also didn't like that the lady had assumed Nat was nothing to him, but he didn't feel the need to share that with her just yet.

Nat laughed. "Yeah, I guess we have been going pretty strong all morning. I suppose you earned yourself a little fun."

He raised one eyebrow. "Well, I have been a very good boy. Exactly how much fun are we talking?"

Nat glared at him but the smile stayed on her lips. "Not that much fun."

Eric stuck his lip out in an exaggerated pout. "Well, I think I have at least earned a coffee break. You don't plan on working me all day, do you?"

"The thought has crossed my mind. We need to get this done. Gina's been doing a good job running the truck while I've been tied up with you but the sooner we get you up and running the sooner I can give her a little break."

"Oh come on. A fifteen-minute break isn't going to kill you. A little caffeine and sugar would go a long way to shutting me up."

Nat snorted. "Fine. I'll feed you."

"Great!" Eric said. "So, where do you want to go?"

"Oh," Nat said with a small frown. "I actually promised Gina I would meet her at one o'clock so she could catch me up on everything going on at the truck."

"So, how about we go to your truck then. I've been meaning to taste these cupcakes you've been crowing over for the last few weeks. I doubt they'll come near to being as good as my aunt's cannoli or baklava was, but I'm willing to give it a shot."

Nat snorted. "Gee, thanks. You certain you want to make that big of a sacrifice? I'm sure we can find you a nice gelato somewhere."

"Ah, Cupcake, don't tease me."

"I wouldn't dream of it."

Eric swallowed, craving a completely different cupcake than the one she was offering. But for the moment, he'd take what he could get. Maybe he could score something chocolate.

He grinned. "Good, it's settled then. Let's get things wrapped up here before my stomach gives up on sustenance and starts eating itself."

Jill came back holding a stack of plates and small saucers. She went to hand them to Eric but he waved them over to Nat. "Better give them to the boss lady. She makes all the important decisions."

Nat rolled her eyes but took the plates.

"We didn't have anything with just leaves or vines on it," Jill said. "But I found these that I thought you might like."

There were about eight different designs of old plates, all with some sort of old floral or toile pattern on them.

"Okay, call me crazy, but what if we went with all of them?" Nat asked.

"Yes, you're crazy," Eric said with a small frown.

"No, really. You want to go for an old-world feel, right? Well what could be more old-world Tuscan country villa than antique country plates?"

"But none of them match."

"I know, but that makes it even more perfect. It'll be an eclectic blend of old-world charm."

She went on and on, painting such a complete picture of an old Tuscan villa that even Eric started to pick up some enthusiasm for the idea. His vision of an upscale teahouse-type bakery was fading more every minute, but in the face of

Natalie's excitement, he found it hard to care.

He sighed. "All right."

"Yes?"

"Yes."

Her smile shattered the last of his reservations. Nothing that could create a smile like that could be wrong. Right?

Jill looked between them, her fake smile warming a few degrees. "You two are definitely meant for each other. How many sets do you need?"

"Actually," Eric said, "we won't need the whole setting, just the plate and the salad plate. As many as you've got."

Jill's eyes widened at that. She glanced down at the inventory sheet in her hand. "Looks like between all the designs there we've got thirty-seven settings."

"Is it possible to just get the plates and salad plates instead of the whole setting?" Nat asked.

"I believe so."

"Great, we'll take all thirty-seven plates and salad plates then," Eric said. "We can come back for them later. Is four o'clock good?"

"No, wait. We just need thirty-six. Thanks," Nat said.

Eric frowned at her. Jill looked back and forth between them and Eric shrugged. "Just thirty-six then, I guess. Four o'clock okay?"

Jill nodded. "That should be fine."

"Great. Thanks." Eric grabbed Nat's hand and pulled her out before she could say anything else.

He was surprised when she didn't pull away once they left the store.

Nat laughed suddenly, an odd little sound that reminded him of an old cat wheezing for breath. "That poor saleswoman. I think we confused her."

"Well, she's probably not used to her customers ordering three dozen place settings at a time."

Nat laughed again. "Probably."

"Speaking of which. Why just the thirty-six settings? We could have used another one and now the store just has one place setting."

Nat shrugged. "Thirty-six just sounded better."

Eric's eyebrow rose. That didn't sound better. Leaving one place setting behind was beyond odd.

Nat suddenly pulled short. Just up ahead was the glaring pink and green truck. Gina was already hanging out of the truck window waving at them. Nat quietly slipped her hand from his and glanced up at him.

"Better go over and say hi."

Eric didn't say anything but followed her over to the truck. Gina glanced back and forth between them, an appraising eyebrow raised.

"How are you two doing today?" she asked.

"Fine," Nat said. "How's business going?"

Gina waved at a handful of people munching on cupcakes nearby. "Good, as always. What have you guys been up to?"

"We were just out shopping for things for the bakery."

"I can see that. Getting much done, are you?"

Eric frowned. She wasn't saying anything untoward, but her tone implied she suspected something other than retail therapy was going on. Of course, it probably only bothered him because he both hoped and feared she was right.

"Yeah," he said. "Natalie's dragged me from one end of this town to the other. The bakery should be fully stocked and loaded by the end of the night, the way we're going. Just stopped off and got some plates. Though she'd only let me buy thirty-six of the thirty-seven settings they had."

Natalie shot him a dirty look and stepped a little farther from him. Eric frowned again, not liking the distance she put between them.

Gina snorted. "Yeah, Nat doesn't like odd numbers."

Eric's eyes widened and he turned to Nat with a grin. "What?"

She tried to wave him off, but Gina jumped back in. "Oh yeah. Follow her around the grocery store sometime. It's fascinating. She'll never buy an odd number of apples. She usually goes for six because four is too few and eight is too many and she'd never, ever buy five or seven."

Eric chuckled. "So does this only apply to apples or anything?"

"Anything. Everything."

"Wait, though, we bought nine table and chair sets at the antique store. That's an odd number."

Gina's eyebrow went up again, her lips pinched together to keep from full-on smiling. She looked at Nat, so Eric turned to her as well, waiting for her to answer.

"It's divisible by three," she murmured, so low he almost didn't hear her.

"What?" Eric said, laughing.

Nat sighed. "Nine doesn't bother me. I don't know why, though I assume it's because it's divisible by three so it doesn't feel so…odd."

That had to be the most adorable thing Eric had ever heard. It took all the self-control he had not to burst out laughing. But Nat was blushing so hot he was afraid she'd melt on the spot. Though he did detect a little smile. Good to know she didn't take herself too seriously.

"All right, leave me and my weird little issues alone," she said, giving him a playful push.

"So," Gina said, "do you guys need a little sugar?"

Natalie looked at him. He shrugged his shoulders. "What's good here?"

"Everything," Nat said with a laugh.

Eric looked over the menu. "What is a build-your-own cupcake?"

"That's our most popular option," Nat said. "We've lots of premade cupcakes but you can also order a custom cupcake just how you like it. You pick the flavor of cake you want, what kind of filling, what kind of frosting, and what toppings you'd like."

"Really? That's...pretty cool, actually."

"We think so."

"So, what do you want?" Gina asked.

Eric glanced at the menu options one more time before answering. "I'll take a chocolate cupcake with chocolate ganache filling, chocolate butter cream frosting, and chocolate sprinkles."

This time both girls' eyebrows shot up. "That's a lot of chocolate," Gina said.

Eric shrugged. "What can I say? I love chocolate."

Gina looked back and forth between Eric and Natalie again.

"What?" Eric asked.

"Nothing," she said. "Nat, you want your usual?" she asked with a smile.

Natalie glared at her. "I think I'll stick with plain vanilla today, thanks," Nat said.

"Whatever." Gina turned her back to get their cupcakes ready.

"What's your usual?" Eric asked.

Natalie's cheeks flushed again. "Pretty much the cupcake you ordered. Only I usually top it with Hershey bar shavings or M&M's or Heath bar or...well you get the point."

Eric laughed. "So I guess we've got at least one thing in common."

"More than that, I thought."

Eric stared at Nat, then took a step closer. "Yes, definitely more than that. I wasn't sure you wanted to remember that."

"I wasn't sure either. I don't seem to have a choice about

it, though."

He brushed a stray curl off her cheek, letting his hand rest against her face for a moment. He wished this whole bakery business wasn't between them. He had no idea how to act around her. In usual circumstances he'd be turning on the charm, wining and dining her, making any excuse he could to touch her. He'd grab a hold of her and never let go. But that wasn't something he could do just now. And if he got his way and got his hands on her garage, he'd probably never get the chance.

He opened his mouth to say something but before he could, "Mamma Mia" interrupted him. He silenced the phone, but he wouldn't be able to ignore her indefinitely. The longer he did, the more she'd call.

"I better get going," he said, both saddened and thrilled when Nat's face fell. She wasn't happy he was leaving. Neither was he. Hopefully that was a good thing.

"More errands for your mom?"

He gave her a crooked grin. "Always."

Before he could say anything else Gina cleared her throat. "Order up!"

Eric took his cupcake and glanced back at Natalie, not sure what to say.

"Well," she said.

"Well." They stared at each other a moment, not saying a word. "Well. I guess I'll get going for now. I'll go get my car, pick up the plates, and see you back at the shop tomorrow."

"Okay. Sounds great."

"Gina," Eric said, lifting his cupcake in a mock salute. He turned on his heel, whistling the oompa loompa song from *Willy Wonka & the Chocolate Factory* as he walked away. He had no clue what he was going to do about his growing interest in Natalie Moran. But for the moment, he'd call his mother before she drove him nuts. And then he was going to go home, enjoy his chocolate, and then, go get the plates.

# Chapter Ten

Nat watched Eric walking away and suppressed a sigh. His mother, or rather his inclination for running whenever Mommy Dearest called, was a bit annoying.

"What the hell do you think you're doing?" Gina asked.

Natalie looked up at her in surprise, licking a bit of vanilla frosting off her lip. "What are you talking about?"

"Don't give me that. I saw you two walking down the street holding hands looking like some happy couple fresh off their white picket fence farm. You must be out of your mind."

"I don't know what you mean. We were just goofing off with this salesgirl in the store and we'd just left the shop. He was still holding my hand. I didn't want to be rude and just yank it away."

"Sure. You didn't want to be rude. That's why you let him hold your hand. That's the excuse you want to go with?"

"It's the truth. I don't know what you think is going on."

"Oh, I can see what's going on. The problem is, *you* can't."

"I seriously don't know what you're talking about."

"I know you don't. That's the problem."

"What's the problem? I've slept with the guy. I can't just pretend like I barely know him. Besides, even if I did like him, a little, maybe, it's not that big a deal."

"Of course it's a big deal. He's only being nice to you because he wants to get his hands on that parking spot of yours. And I'm not talking about the one he already got his hands on," Gina said, her gaze flicking to Nat's nether region.

Nat gasped in mock shock and flicked some frosting at Gina. "You did *not* just go there."

"Oh yeah. I did. But focus, please. He needs you to help him get the bakery running, he needs your garage, and until he gets what he wants, of course he's going to be nice to you and flirt a little, buddy up to you real nice so when he goes in for the swoop, you don't put up a fight."

"Sure, because there's no other reason a good-looking, successful man would want me except for what he can get out of me, right?"

"That's not what I meant, and you know it."

Nat took a deep breath. Yeah, she did know that. But still she couldn't help thinking it.

"That is *not* what's going on," Natalie said. "First of all, he's not buttering me up. The man is aggravating in the extreme. All we do is argue about everything. We have nothing in common. We can't agree on anything. You just happened to see the one moment where we were playing around a little. But believe me, this has not been one big flirt-fest. The man is a Class A-1 pain in the ass."

"That you've already slept with."

Nat opened her mouth, then shut it again. Gina's eyebrow went up. Nat sighed. "That was a onetime deal."

"If you say so. All I'm saying is you should be careful. Men are hard enough to trust as it is. But when you've got one that wants something from you, it's especially dangerous. You've already learned that the hard way."

Nat frowned, her blood running cold at the memory of her asshat of an ex. She hadn't thought anything of doing all the work on their cookbook. After all, those might have been her recipes, but he had tested them out for her and he had the connections who were helping get the book published. And they had been engaged. She had figured the money they would earn on the book would go to both of them. Until he'd fallen in love with someone else and had taken the manuscript, along with just about everything else they had co-owned, and left.

She'd put up enough of a fuss that he agreed to pay her half of the advance he'd received if she gave up any further claim to the book. And the only reason she'd taken that crappy deal was to get him out of her life, once and for all. It had given her enough capital to start a new life without him. But being completely used and tossed away by the one person who should have loved her the most had left her extremely wary of trusting anyone again.

But, Eric was nothing like him. Though, granted, Eric had more of a reason to get on her good side than her ex ever had. Which gave him more of an opportunity to betray her.

Suddenly, all the little flirtatious moments that had happened since they'd met seemed less playful. She had been getting more comfortable with him. And she had really enjoyed holding his hand, letting herself touch him. Her body seemed to crave contact with him and giving in to that need, even for a moment, had been heavenly.

Every other word out of his mouth was a sexual innuendo of some kind and it had been fun to play along. But it was one thing to play. It was another thing entirely to get played. She didn't think that's what he was doing, but Eric did want that parking garage and he did need her to get his bakery started. So did that mean the little moments they'd shared were all some part of his grand master plan? The thought depressed

Natalie more than she wanted to admit.

"Don't worry," she said. "I might've been playing around a little but I have no intention of letting him seduce my future out from underneath me."

"Good. I mean, don't get me wrong. Under normal circumstances, I'd tell you to go for it in a heartbeat. That man has got a seriously rocking body. And if you were me, it wouldn't be an issue. Hook up as much as you want and then walk away. But you aren't me so…" Gina shrugged.

"So what?"

"So, you aren't capable of just sleeping with a guy without getting attached. And that's not a bad thing. But I don't want you setting yourself up for a lot of heartache. So just be careful."

Natalie wanted to argue with her but knew she was right. It didn't make it easier to swallow, but still. She sighed. "I will be."

"Good. Now go eat your cupcake. Some of us have to work."

Natalie chucked a chunk of cupcake at her and Gina ducked before winking at Nat and going back to work.

"All right, contain yourself!" Gina said to the guy standing impatiently at the truck window.

Nat laughed and shook her head. Her smile faded though, with Gina's warnings echoing in her head. She knew her friend had a good point. And experience had taught her to be careful. Most of the men she'd dated had used her, cheated on her, or lied to her, with Steve being the crowning glory of them all. She'd given up after him. Eric seemed so different, though. Maybe he was. But, just in case, she'd be wise to keep her distance. If she could.

• • •

"You are out of your fucking mind," Jared said, waving at the bartender to bring him another beer.

Eric took a swig of his own beer and looked at his friend in surprise. "What?"

"Don't give me that look, man. I've known you since high school. You got it bad for this girl."

"I do not. But we do have to work together, so I don't see the point in being a jerk about it."

"She's using you, dude. She wants a piece of what you got and not in a good way."

Eric's eyebrow rose a notch.

"You know what I mean," Jared said.

Eric shook his head. "I don't think I have anything to worry about. She goes out of her way to make sure I know she's not interested in me."

"Whatever. She damn well is interested in you. She wants your business. You think she's putting in all this work just out of the goodness of her heart? She wants you to make her a partner, at the very least. Why else is she working so hard? Just for a few hours in the kitchen?"

Eric frowned. "I don't think she's like that."

"Of course you don't. That's what she wants you to think. She wants you to think she's nothing but a sweet little cupcake baker who's just doing her good deed for the day. And then when she's got you so dependent on her that you can't run the place without her, *that's* when she forces your hand."

"Forces my hand on what?"

"She wants a piece of that bakery. She's already got your parking garage. You let her be a partner and she pretty much owns two thirds of the place. And if she's the one that gets things up and running, well then, there's not much need for you, is there? At best, you'll be a silent partner and at worst…"

"At worst, I won't be there at all."

"You said it, man." Jared shrugged and took another swig

of his beer.

Eric slowly drank his beer, his eyes on the screen in front of him, though he wasn't watching the game at all. He didn't think Natalie was that conniving. Sure, she did know how to get under his skin until he didn't know what to do and he was always on the verge of either pulling his hair out or shoving her up against a wall and kissing her until she was breathless and begging for him. As for the control thing, she couldn't seem to help herself. Organization was like her drug of choice.

But she did seem to change gears kind of quickly. One moment she would be arguing with him until she was blue in the face, and the next she was flirtatiously playing with him. He guessed Jared had a point. But the thought didn't make him happy.

"I don't know. She's never said anything about becoming partners, never acted like she was more than helping me out. She knows I'm never going to give up the bakery."

"Does she? Think about it, man. This is something you decided to do on the spur of the moment because someone handed the building to you. It's not something you would have necessarily chosen to do. In her mind, it's probably something you wouldn't care about walking away from. So, if she gets her hooks in real deep, she probably figures maybe it'll be easy for you to walk away. Face it, she is getting the short end of the stick in your little deal."

"No she's not. She's getting everything she wanted."

"What, she gets to use your kitchen for a couple hours a day and make your deliveries for you? Yeah, I'm sure that's what she always wanted. And in exchange, she sets up your bakery for you. Hopefully, it becomes successful, which is something she's probably always wanted, and then what? She just walks away? How does that make any kind of sense?"

Eric opened his mouth to argue but paused. It *didn't* make any sense. Yes, using his kitchen saved her some fees but was the money she saved really worth all the work she was putting in to start up *his* bakery?

Eric downed the rest of his beer and pushed back from the bar. A slow headache had formed behind his eyes.

Jared looked at him. "You calling it a night?"

"Yeah. It's been a long day."

"Look, man, I hope you know I'm just looking out for you. I'm not saying she's not a genuinely nice girl. She might be. I'm just saying, be careful."

"I will be," Eric said. "You still coming in tomorrow to start learning the ropes?"

Jared frowned. "Since you won't let up on the guilt trip until I do, I guess so."

"I'm not guilt-tripping you."

"Ha!" Jared drained his beer and slammed the bottle down. "What was all that 'I need some help down there,' and 'you don't have anything else going on right now' and 'I'd do it for you' shit you've been feeding me."

"Well, it's not a guilt trip, if it's true." Eric laughed at Jared's scowl. "Ah, come on. It won't be that bad. Is earning a few bucks for an honest day's work really such a horrifying concept?"

Jared shivered. "You're damn right it is."

Eric laughed again and slung his jacket over his shoulders. "I promise it won't hurt. Not even a little."

"Whatever you say, man."

"See you later," Eric said, heading for the exit.

By the time he'd reached the door, his amusement over Jared's reluctance to work had drowned in the sea of his warnings against Nat. Eric pushed the door open and went into the night, taking a deep breath to clear his slightly fuzzy head. He knew Jared made a lot of sense. But he didn't like it. At all.

# Chapter Eleven

Nat walked into the bakery refreshed, for once, because she'd been able to sleep in that morning. Between her getting the truck ready in the mornings and Gina running it full time while she'd been working for Eric, Nat and Gina had decided a break was in order, so they'd taken the weekend off. Plus, the guy she'd paid to fix Eric's car had offered her a deal on touching up her truck so with the cupcake business on a break, it was a good time to give the truck a face-lift. Which reminded her, she still needed to replace the shirt she'd ruined. There was no way even the dry cleaner was getting chocolate gelato out of the one he'd been wearing.

Regardless, Nat was now fully awake and ready to deal with Eric. She immediately scanned the kitchen for signs of tampering. And just as she thought, he'd done it again. She huffed and marched over to the counter where the jars of whisks, spatulas, and mixing spoons were stored. When she'd left the night before, each jar had contained eight of each utensil. Now, they were completely mixed together. And she knew if she counted, there'd be an odd number of each utensil in each jar.

"I can't believe he is so juvenile," she muttered while she set about reorganizing everything.

She kept up the tirade while she inspected the rest of the kitchen and set to rights whatever Eric had messed up, trying to keep her anger nice and stoked until he wandered in. The problem was, she found it kind of funny. It had turned into a game. Like hide and seek. Or lying in bed before Christmas morning trying to guess what was waiting for you under the tree. She never knew what would be waiting for her when she walked in the bakery and she hated to admit it, but she kind of looked forward to finding out every day.

Last week, she'd come in to find all the spices out of order and shoved in random spots around the room. And yesterday, he'd moved all the motivational pictures she'd hung on the walls in the kitchen. He'd apparently noticed that she'd hung the pictures in alphabetical order. Believe, Confidence, Excellence, Motivation, Potential, and so on. He'd rearranged them all. And made sure they hung just slightly crooked. Even she had to admit that was kind of genius.

Nat had finally started striking back. She'd changed his "Stud Muffin" apron to one that read Kitchen Bitch in hot pink lettering. And she had something extra special waiting for him in the freezer. He'd finally wrapped up enough loose ends to start his vacation time and was a full-time bakery owner for the time being. To celebrate, he'd purchased a special treat. He'd be in any minute so they could get going on painting the front but he wouldn't be able to resist a quick snack.

The back door opened and Eric and Jared sauntered in. Eric saw what she was doing and grinned.

"How's it going, Cupcake?"

"Just fine, Gelato."

"Good to hear it. Doing a little rearranging?"

Nat smiled at him. "Straightening up. Things were a bit odd when I came in."

Eric's grin grew wider. "*Hmm*, that *is* odd."

Jared looked back and forth between them. "You two are odd."

Nat and Eric just beamed at him until he frowned and wandered away, muttering something about people needing to up their dosages.

Nat laughed and finished with the spoons. "You ready to get to work?" she asked, pulling her hair back into a messy bun.

"In just a minute." Eric grabbed a teaspoon out of a drawer and went to the freezer. "I am my own boss for the next three months. And I am going to celebrate."

He took a pint of his favorite milk chocolate gelato from the freezer and held it out to her. "Care to join me?"

Nat waved him off. "No, thanks. You earned that. Enjoy."

"I will," he said, winking at her. He followed Jared into the front room and settled down on the floor.

Nat leaned back against the counter, her arms folded, a smile already on her face. "Five…four…three…two…one…"

"Natalie!"

She broke into a full-toothed grin and poked her head out of the kitchen. Eric was standing, holding the pint away from him like it was a snake about to strike. A large blob of the stuff lay on the floor at his feet with more of it dribbling down his chin.

"Yes, Eric?"

He looked at her, his mouth hanging open. "What the hell did you do?"

She blinked innocently. "Oh nothing. I just thought you should have something extra special to celebrate with so I went to that garlic bistro and picked up a pint. I paid a bit more to have a little extra flavor mixed in. It was a little more expensive, of course, but nothing is too good for you," she said, batting her eyelashes at him.

He wiped a hand across his mouth. "And exactly what flavor is this?"

"Garlic and anchovy."

"What?" he shrieked.

Nat grinned wider. "Payback's a bitch, baby."

"Oh, you are so going to pay!" Eric dropped the ice cream and lunged for her.

Nat shrieked and ran laughing into the kitchen but Eric was hot on her heels. There really wasn't anywhere to run. He had her pinned against the sink in under ten seconds. He scooped a bit of the ice cream off his shirt.

"If I had to eat it, you do, too," he said, trying to get the stuff in her mouth.

She shrieked again and tried to dodge his hands, though it was hard to keep her mouth closed when she was laughing so hard she could barely breathe. He managed to get a little in and she immediately spit it back out.

"Oh my God," she laughed, "that is truly foul."

"Ha! Serves you right, defiling my gelato like that."

"It's better than putting vegetable oil in my glass cleaning solution! That was just mean. I still can't get the streaks off that mirror in the bathroom."

Eric chuckled and held on tighter when she squirmed to get away. "Okay, okay. I call a truce."

Nat stopped squirming. "You mean it?"

"I mean it. I'll stop messing with everything around the kitchen, if you promise you will never, ever touch my gelato."

She laughed and nodded. "Okay, fine, I agree."

"Good," Eric said. But he still didn't let her go.

They were breathing hard from their mock battle and both of them suddenly realized they were molded together, from hip to chest, their arms locked around each other, their chests heaving in unison with every ragged breath they took.

Eric's gaze met hers and he leaned in, slow enough that she could pull away if she wanted. She should. The smart thing to do would be to push him away. But since when did her body ever listen to what was smart when it came to Eric?

She tilted her head up and closed the distance between them. The second their lips met, Eric crushed her to him with a groan and Nat clung to him for dear life. There was no soft build up. Just raw need. They hadn't touched each other, aside from the handholding, since that night at his house and judging by the way Eric was kissing her, he'd been missing her as badly as she had him. She opened to him, whimpering when his tongue invaded her mouth. She wrapped her arms around his neck, fisting her hands in his hair to keep him pinned to her lips. Sweet balls of fire, if he stopped kissing her now she'd die on the spot.

"Good God, get a room." Gina's voice was like a bucket of ice water and Eric and Nat broke apart like two guilty teenagers who'd been caught making out by their mom.

"I thought we were here to paint, not watch you two commit three major health code violations."

"I don't see why we can't do both," Jared said.

Nat gasped and turned to find Jared leaning against the doorframe. Blood rushed to her cheeks so quickly it made her head spin and she buried her face against Eric's chest.

"All right, show's over," Eric said, though he didn't sound nearly as outraged as he should have.

Gina shook her head and headed for the front of the bakery, pushing Jared ahead of her as she went.

Nat looked up at Eric and he grinned down at her. She glared at him. He laughed and let go of her, stepping back so she could move away from the sink.

"Sorry, I suppose I should apologize," he said. "But I've wanted to do that for weeks. And unless you are a very good actress, I think you wanted it, too."

Nat blushed again but she didn't deny it. It would be kind of pointless to do that after she'd tried to get him to swallow her tonsils.

She sighed. "Yes, I did. But while I enjoyed that…"

Eric reached out to stroke her cheek and Nat had to step away from his touch to keep from launching herself at him again.

"I just don't think it's a good idea for us to get involved. Right now."

Eric sighed and dropped his hand. "I know."

"You do?" It was what she'd wanted him to say. So why did she feel so disappointed?

"Yeah. Mixing business and pleasure is never a good idea. So I've heard, anyway," he said with a small smile. "However…"

"However…" Nat echoed.

Eric shrugged. "I've never been great with rules. And to be honest, I want you so damn much it's getting hard to be around you."

Nat's eyebrow shot up and she aimed a very determined look at his crotch. Eric laughed.

"Yes, that pun was totally intended."

Nat smiled and stepped back to lay her head on Eric's chest. She took a deep breath, sighing when his arms came around her.

"Okay," he said, pulling back from his embrace. "How about this? We put a pin on…whatever this is. For now. Until the bakery is up and running and we've got the rest of our… business association all straightened out. And then, we can figure out where to go from there."

Nat nodded, fighting her disappointment. It was the smart thing to do. That didn't mean she had to like it. "All right. We can just be friends for now."

"Friends?"

The quirked eyebrow did her in. Damn, why did he have to be so insanely sexy? "Good friends?"

"*Hmm*," Eric said, his grip tightening. "I like that idea."

"Not like that," Nat said, laughing as she pushed away from him. "We've sort of done everything backward. Jumped into bed before we knew each other. So, why don't we just slow it down a little and start from the beginning?"

"As friends, huh?"

"For now. And then we'll see how it goes from there."

Eric gave her a small smile. "I suppose we can try that."

"Good. Well then," Nat said, stepping away from him. "I think we've got some painting to do."

"Oh, about that…" Eric said, following her into the front room.

Nat stopped short and stared down at the supplies Jared had spread out in the middle of the room. Five gallons of paint and seven rollers. She turned to Eric and folded her arms. "Seriously?"

Eric gave her a sheepish grin. "I got the supplies before our truce. It's going to be a hard habit to break but I'll try, I swear."

Nat sighed, but couldn't stop a small smile from peeking through. The man was going to be the death of her. And going by the warmth and little prickles of excitement that were spreading through her at just the sight of him, she was going to go to her grave enjoying every second of it.

# Chapter Twelve

Natalie did a last touch-up on her makeup and made a face at herself in the mirror. Not too bad. The party was Gatsby-themed and she'd gotten hold of an absolutely gorgeous black beaded and fringed dress. She'd tucked her hair into a black, straight-bobbed wig, and for once she'd managed to pull off a nice smoky-eye look. Usually, when she attempted it, she ended up looking like someone had beaten her with a bag of nickels. But she looked pretty damn good, if she did say so herself.

The dress had come with a rhinestone headdress sporting a gorgeous peacock feather and she added a long gold necklace that swayed tantalizingly between her breasts. She was ready to get her party on.

It had been a long couple of weeks since she and Eric had vowed to take things slow and focus on work. The daily urge to rip his clothes off and get their freak on was getting exhausting. She still thought it was a good idea, though. They already knew they had sexual chemistry. Probably too much. But Nat wanted to make sure they actually liked each other, not just liked sleeping together. She was not going to have a repeat of her last disastrous relationship.

So tonight, Nat was looking forward to cutting loose and just having a good time without having to worry about dealing with Eric and her inexplicable feelings for him. Her friend's birthday party was a great excuse to get all dolled up and have some fun.

"You ready yet?" Gina asked. She, of course, looked like a total knockout in a mini red fringed dress.

Nat stood and spun around. "What do you think?"

Gina whistled. "I think every man there will be drooling all over you within half a second of seeing you."

"Just what I was going for," Nat said, laughing.

"Well, it might not be a bad idea if you met someone tonight. It'd get your mind off you-know-who."

"Who?" Nat asked, playing totally dumb. So much for not bringing him up tonight.

"Seriously?" Gina rolled her eyes. "Your Gelato man."

"My mind is not on him."

"Whatever. Your mind is always on him. I've never seen you so hooked on a guy before and under normal circumstances, I'd be thrilled for you. I mean the guy is gorgeous and rich, two of my favorite things. But with your special little situation…"

Nat frowned. "What do you mean, rich? He's just a junior financial consultant at a tiny firm. And if all goes according to his plan, he'll be a self-employed owner of a bakery that isn't even open yet."

"Didn't you Google him?"

Nat shook her head and Gina rolled her eyes again. "Good God girl, that's the first thing I do when I meet a new guy. Your boy is the son of Jerry and Miranda Schneider. They own like half the city."

Nat frowned. She'd known he was fairly successful. He'd

have to be to live in the place he did, but she hadn't known he was *that* well off. "If he's got that much money, why doesn't he just buy me out? Or try to, anyway?"

Gina shrugged and leaned down to look in the mirror so she could touch up her lipstick. "I don't know. But he's not working for mommy and daddy and he did have an actual job, so he's not some trust fund baby. Or a really bad one, anyway. Maybe he got cut off or something."

Nat let that info churn around in her head for a second. The rich parents would explain Eric's house. But everything else about him screamed "normal person," not rich spoiled brat. And if he had access to mommy and daddy's millions he surely would have offered to buy her out of their joint inheritance. Instead, he had seemed genuinely dismayed at how much it would cost to do that. He certainly didn't act like someone who had that kind of money lying around. As his parents most certainly did.

Maybe he *had* been cut off, or maybe he was trying to live life on his own terms. If that was the case, that made her like him even more. Great, just what she needed. Even more reasons to fall head over heels for the guy.

"You ready?" Gina asked again.

"Yeah, just a sec," Nat said, putting her makeup away and straightening up the desk.

"Has Eric let up on messing with your stuff?" Gina asked.

"Mostly. But he's still always messing up the spices so I have to re-alphabetize them every day. He swears he's not doing it on purpose but I know he is."

"Yeah, well, alphabetizing everything that isn't nailed down drives everyone nuts, Nat. Can't really blame him on that one."

Nat huffed. "I really don't understand what everyone has against organization. Anyway," she said, drawing out the word until Gina drew an invisible zipper across her lips, "he's stopped moving the utensils so there are odd piles everywhere but he hides my favorite whisk, you know that big pink one? He swears he's not doing it, but I find it in the weirdest places. Like the freezer. Or in the planter. And, he hates my oven mitts!"

Gina burst out laughing at that one. "They *are* hideous."

Nat mock-gasped. "They are awesome! Wait...which ones?" She'd been collecting oven mitts for years and had a truly spectacular and unique collection.

"All of them. Especially that pair that looks like that Spat guy."

"Spat?"

"You know, from Star Trails. Spat...Sport...Spit..."

"Star Trek? My Spock mitts? Those are so cool! They look like Spock doing the *live long and prosper* sign. Who could hate those?"

"Uh-huh. I'm just sayin', give the guy a break over the mitts. It takes a very special person to love those things." She patted Nat's head like she was an eccentric pet and then jumped up.

"And I've gotta be honest, I mess with you and your numbers and organizing stuff, too. Kinda makes me like the guy better."

Nat gasped again and chucked a hairbrush at her friend, deliberately missing, of course.

"All right, enough of that. We've got better things to do tonight than worry about the biggest pain in your ass at the moment. You ready to go?"

This was an Eric-free evening so Nat tried to put thoughts of him out of her head. No tension, no arguing, no drooling, and no chance of being seduced out of her very willing panties at just a look from him. It was going to be nice to have some fun and not have to keep her guard up.

She grabbed the shawl that went with the dress and

wrapped it around her shoulders. "Yep, let's go!"

The party was only a couple blocks from their own building, so Nat and Gina hoofed it. The second they walked in the door, Gina pulled her over to the liquor table and pressed a glass of wine into her hand.

"Here you go," she said. "This will help loosen you up a bit."

Nat laughed and took a sip. "Just being away from baking and the bakery is already doing wonders. Wow," she said, looking around the loft. "This place looks amazing!"

All the furniture had been arranged around the periphery of the room, leaving a large space in the middle where a makeshift dance floor had been set up. The apartment had been draped in glittering beads and metallic drapes, mirrored surfaces everywhere. Catering staff in tuxedos wandered around with trays heaped with delicious-looking food and another table near the kitchen was groaning under the weight of a huge art deco birthday cake and more finger foods.

Nat snagged some sort of cream puff from a passing waiter and popped it in her mouth, nearly groaning in ecstasy as the sugary custard filled her mouth. "Oh my God, that is so good," she said.

Gina didn't hear her though. Her attention was focused on something across the room.

"What are you looking at?" Nat asked.

Gina grimaced. "Well, if you came here to escape Eric, you might not want to look over by the terrace."

Natalie spun around. Eric stood leaning near the open terrace door looking absolutely mouthwatering in a dark pinstriped suit. He'd even added a little twenties-style mustache. Nat was not a fan of facial hair, but damn, Eric pulled it off. She took another sip of her wine, though the tingles spreading through her had nothing to do with alcohol. There was no escaping the man. It might make it a little easier if her body wasn't so obviously thrilled to see him. His fingers played with the rim of his glass and her nipples tightened into hard little buds of desire, emanating tiny shocks of electricity through her body every time the silky fabric she wore moved over them.

"Who the hell is that?" Gina asked, nodding at the woman Eric was talking to.

Nat hadn't even noticed her. Which was hard to believe considering that all his attention was focused on the tall, leggy blonde. And he looked like he was having a great time.

"I have no idea."

Gina snorted. "Typical. Of course he latches onto the blonde Barbie with the big boobs."

Nat frowned. The woman was the exact opposite of her in nearly every way. Fake boobs, fake teeth, fake hair, dripping in what looked like very real diamonds. Obviously, someone who would fit right in at his parents' country club. Nat shook her head, ashamed at her instant judgment of the woman.

"She might be a perfectly nice person," Nat said, trying her damnedest to be fair. She tore her gaze from them. It would be a lot easier if she didn't have to watch Eric flirting with her.

"Yeah, well that perfectly nice person is hanging all over your boy," Gina pointed out.

"He's not my anything, Gina. We just work together. Temporarily."

"*Um-hmm*," Gina said, obviously not buying that one. "Hang on a sec."

Nat popped another cream puff while Gina performed a little light recon, chatting with one person or another with a few nods in Eric's direction before she made her way back to Natalie.

"Her name is Courtney Collins."

"Courtney?" Nat wondered if it was the same Courtney

he'd had to pick up from the airport. From the way she was hanging on him, she certainly seemed like a close friend. *Very* close.

"Yep. She's been after Schneider for years. And from the looks of it, she might be making some progress."

Nat turned back to the terrace, unable to keep from looking. Courtney had put her hand on Eric's arm, laughing hysterically at something he was saying. The hand crept up a little higher, resting on his bicep. Eric did nothing to move away from her.

"Bitch," Nat muttered under her breath.

She sighed and forced herself to turn her back on Big Boobs and Bozo.

So much for taking it slow and getting to know one another before building a relationship. Apparently, they'd been taking it a little too slow. Not that they'd ever said they were exclusive. Or even dating. But still. It hurt.

Well. She was going to enjoy her night, no matter what was going on near the balcony. She was in a room full of friends she hadn't seen in weeks, had an excellent glass of wine in her hand, her favorite tunes were playing, and there was a table full of junk food in the kitchen. She did her best to put Eric from her mind and went to mingle.

• • •

Eric kept the grin plastered on his face, trying his best to look interested at the inane drivel pouring from Courtney's mouth. If she wasn't the daughter of his father's business partner, Eric would have bailed on her after the first word had left her mouth. She was gorgeous—most guys' wet dreams just waiting to happen. And Eric knew she had a brain in her head. The girl had gone to Harvard, for shit's sake. But for some reason, every time they got within ten feet of each other, she turned into a giggling airhead who made Eric want to gouge his ears out. As far as he could tell, it was Court's version of flirting. The only thing it made him want to do was take a flying leap off the balcony.

While Courtney babbled on about the latest scandal at their parents' country club, Eric let his eyes roam over the crowd. Maybe he'd get lucky and find someone he knew who could rescue him. He'd only come to see an old school friend of his, the boyfriend of the birthday girl. So far, he hadn't seen anyone else he knew well. A few acquaintances (he winced at a particularly loud giggle from Courtney) but no one else he really cared to spend the evening making small talk with.

Still, he'd promised his friend he'd make an appearance and for the time and money he'd put into his authentic twenties suit, he was bound and determined to stick it out for at least another half hour. Though, a few more minutes with Courtney and he might just run screaming from the building, no matter how much the damn suit he was wearing had cost to rent.

One of his favorite Parov Stelar songs came on and Eric itched to get out on the dance floor. How rude would Courtney think he was, if he just handed her his glass and walked away? She'd probably complain to her mother who would complain to his mother who would call him and chew him out for the better part of an afternoon. Not worth the trouble. He sighed and took another drink.

Then he heard a laugh that he'd recognize anywhere. He looked over Courtney's shoulder, leaning over a bit to get a better view. Someone spun out of the way, and there she was. Natalie. Spinning and shaking that seriously sweet ass of hers, laughing as she and Gina bounced together to the music.

"Excuse me," Eric said, pressing his glass into Courtney's hand, barely hearing her squeak of protest.

He pushed through the crowd on the makeshift dance

floor until he was close enough to touch her. He reached out and grabbed her hand. She jerked, her look of alarm fading into one of annoyance when she saw him. *Hmm*. What had he done to piss her off between leaving the bakery and showing up here? He hadn't even spoken to her. Not that he was going to let her obvious irritation stop him. She was the only one he'd wanted to see tonight and his luck in finding her here was too good to pass up.

"You look amazing." He let his gaze wander over her again. The dress hugged her in all the right places, the fringe moving tantalizingly with every breath she took. "I didn't know you'd be here," he said, pulling her a little closer to talk in her ear so she could hear him.

"You didn't ask."

True. Okay, new tactic. "Having a good time?"

"I was."

Irritation of his own started to bleed over his happiness at seeing her. "Did I do something to piss you off? Recently, I mean?"

Her lips twitched. Eric leaned down a bit, making her keep eye contact with him, and her smile spread a little wider. He laced his fingers with hers. That was better. He spun her out a bit and pulled her back in, his blood pulsing with the beat of the music and the memory of the last time they'd been on the dance floor together. The hope for a repeat performance had his heart pounding in his chest, straining toward Nat.

So far, so good. She let him pull her closer, started to sway with him. And then she froze, her gaze fixed over his shoulder. She pushed away from him.

"What's wrong?" he asked.

"I think your date wants you."

"She's not my date. And I want to dance with *you*."

He grabbed her hand and spun her out, then pulled her back to him with a twirl. She squeaked in surprise, a little laugh escaping her kissable lips before she could stop it. God, but she was adorable. If they weren't surrounded by people, he'd lock those long legs of hers around his waist and keep her there until those giggles turned to cries of pure pleasure.

"Come on, Cupcake," he said, wrapping his arm around her waist and dipping her low. He placed his lips close to her ear and whispered, "Dance with me."

He brought her back up, his hand on the small of her back, keeping her pressed tightly to him. Nat narrowed her eyes but they glowed warm like drops of amber in sunlight. She draped an arm around his neck and started to sway with him. He spun with her, faster and faster in time to the music, twirling her out, back to his chest, out to the other side, until the people around them began to step back and give them room to really move.

Nat's smile stretched from ear to ear and she let go and really got into it. Eric's blood pounded through his body, his heart thumping along with the beat, his eyes only on Nat as she moved with him. He grasped her around the waist and hoisted her up, swinging her from one side of his body to the other, then over his head. She planted her hands on his shoulders and kicked her legs into the air.

Eric never thought he'd thank his mother for those dance classes she insisted he take, but the swing dancing lessons were certainly paying off. He brought Nat back down and wrapped his arm around her again, keeping her close to him while the song wound down. She was breathless with laughter and exertion.

"Where did you learn to dance like that?"

"My education was very thorough," he said, winking at her.

She laughed again. "Apparently."

The song ended and Natalie stepped away from him to clap along with the others. He instantly missed her warmth against him and wanted to pull her back. Before he could, Nat's expression changed subtly. The smile stayed in place but seemed more brittle, forced, no longer reaching her eyes.

He knew what was wrong before the problem at hand spoke.

"That was very entertaining, Eric. You certainly don't disappoint when you say you're going to show a girl a good time."

Eric turned to Courtney, surprised at the strength of the anger that coursed through him.

"I never said that, Courtney."

"Well, not in so many words, but you did promise your mother you'd keep me amused for the evening."

His gaze flicked to Nat whose smile had almost entirely disappeared.

"That's not quite what I—"

"You don't mind if I steal him back now, do you?" Courtney asked Nat.

Eric opened his mouth to protest but Nat beat him to it. "He's all yours," she said.

"Nat, wait," he said, but she had already disappeared into the crowd. Before he could go after her, Courtney pressed a tumbler into his hand.

"I got you a fresh drink," she said.

"Thanks," he mumbled, his eyes still searching through the throng of people dancing and chatting. "If you'll excuse me…"

"Oh no, mister. Not this time. Your mother promised me you'd pay attention to me tonight. Besides, there are a few people here you must meet."

Courtney grabbed his hand and towed him off the dance floor toward the den. Eric caught sight of Nat again near the door and he pulled his hand free from Courtney's grasp. Nat looked over at him, their eyes locking for a brief moment before her gaze flicked to Courtney. She frowned. Gina came over, handed her a shawl, and opened the door. She paused just long enough to shoot him a glare before they pulled the door closed behind them.

He started toward the door, meaning to follow her and find out what the hell was going on in her head, make sure she knew that Courtney was nothing but a nuisance he had to put up with, but the nuisance in question put her hand on his arm.

"Eric, I'd like you to meet..." Eric didn't even hear the guy's name. His mind was still focused on Nat.

Nat was definitely peeved about Courtney, which both confused Eric and thrilled him at the same time. He wasn't sure why she cared. She'd made it very clear she didn't want a relationship with him right now. They were friends. With the potential for something more, sure. But just friends, all the same. Though if she was jealous, maybe she *was* ready for something more between them. Which was a thought he very much enjoyed. Though, trying to figure out what the hell was going on in her head was making *his* head throb.

It took several more minutes to extricate himself from Courtney and her throng, and by the time he did, Nat was long gone. With her not there, Eric had no desire to be either. He made his excuses to the hosts and grabbed his jacket, slipping out the door when Courtney's back was turned.

Maybe a nice long walk would help clear his head. Natalie burned so hot and cold Eric had no fucking clue what to do about her. Their night together more than a month ago had proven she was more than hot for him. It hadn't just been sex. But what it was, exactly, he wasn't sure.

His dad's lawyer had discovered some mess with Nat's ex that had both his parents on red alert. After Nat and her ex had broken up, her ex had published a cookbook that Nat had insisted was hers. Only she didn't fight to get her name on the cover. According to the info his dad had, she'd just wanted money. Once her ex had ponied up some cash, she'd dropped the whole thing. Eric wasn't sure what to make of it.

On the one hand, he couldn't imagine Nat trying to claim something that wasn't hers. On the other, if she had been the true author, why wouldn't she fight to get her name on the cover? Or at least credit as a contributor? Why take what was a ridiculously small settlement compared to what the book had since made? None of it made any sense to him.

But there was something between them he'd never felt before. Something he couldn't ignore. Yet, she'd spent every day since then making sure they kept as much distance between them as possible. Except for the brief moments when she couldn't seem to help herself. After which, she had pumped the brakes even harder. If she was angry over him being at a party with another woman...maybe she *did* want to take it to the next level.

He sure as hell hoped so. And he was damn well going to find out.

# Chapter Thirteen

Natalie watched Eric tie the apron around his waist, admiring the way the fabric hugged his toned body. When he looked up she hurriedly glanced at the wall, not wanting to be caught staring.

She'd been keeping her distance since the party, but after only two days she knew she wouldn't be able to maintain it. And she didn't even want to, if she was honest with herself. She didn't know what Eric had been doing with that woman at the party. But she also had no right to get her panties in a wad about it. They weren't even dating, let alone exclusive. She'd keep her eyes open. But punishing him for talking to some other girl wasn't exactly fair. Besides, it was too hard trying to work with him and stay mad at him at the same time.

"You know," he said, "I don't really need baking lessons. We've been cleaning this place all day. I don't know why you want to mess it all up again. I mean, I know I botched the job last night but I probably just misread something. All you have to do is follow the recipe, right?"

"Well, I would've thought so." She glanced at the pile of

burned cupcakes on the counter. "But something obviously went very, very wrong. I said make a dozen cupcakes. Not hockey pucks," she said, whacking one against the countertop.

Eric grimaced and if she didn't know better, she could swear that he blushed. But he turned away before she could see for sure. All right, maybe she'd give him a break and let up a little. She tried hard to keep a straight face. Maybe he was just bad at following directions. Because really, it wasn't that hard to follow a recipe. You read it and then do what it says. But apparently, it wasn't that easy. For some people.

"Yeah, well, like I said, obviously something went a little wonky last night. But that doesn't mean it'll happen again. I mean how hard can this be?"

"I guess we'll find out, won't we?"

Eric rolled his eyes but turned to the counter where the ingredients were laid out. "All right, boss lady. What do I do first?"

"What does the recipe say?"

"I thought the point of having you here was so I didn't have to read the recipe. If I have to read it anyway, why can't I just do this on my own?"

"I don't know. Why can't you?" She tried to keep a laugh in but didn't quite succeed. The sound erupted in a little snort and she slapped her hand over her mouth and turned away.

"Ha ha, yeah, very funny." His tone was irritated but his lips were twitching as well. He sighed. "All right, fine."

He pulled the recipe toward him and ran a finger down the page as he read. If his lips started moving, Nat was totally going to lose it. She tamped down her amusement and tried to look helpful.

"Okay. So what does it tell you to do first?"

"It says to add the butter."

"Okay. Go get it."

Eric's eyes narrowed but he went to the fridge and

grabbed a box of butter. Natalie frowned.

"What? I can't have possibly screwed up already. I haven't done anything yet."

"It says to add softened butter."

"Okay. Well, can't I just throw it in the microwave for a minute?"

"Yes. But it's hard to gauge how soft it's getting. It needs to be soft, not melted, or it'll throw off the consistency of your whole recipe. It's better to use butter that has been on the counter so it's at room temperature. There's a dish of it over there," she said, pointing at a covered bowl near his elbow.

He grabbed the bowl and a measuring cup and started spooning some into the cup. Only instead of leveling it out, Eric heaped lumps of it into the cup and went to dump it inside the mixing bowl.

"Wait." Natalie came over to him and put her hand around his, helping him hold the cup steady. She took a spoon and pressed the butter into the cup. "See. You have to make sure it's completely full and level. Otherwise you may not be getting the correct amount and it will—"

"I know, I know. Throw off my recipe."

She glared at him but without any real heat. "Yeah, that's right."

God, he smelled good. She wasn't sure what cologne he was wearing, or if it was just a particularly enticing brand of soap, but it made her want to shove her nose into the hollow of his throat and inhale deeply. Maybe hang out there long enough to take a taste. Or two. She licked her lips and looked up to find Eric staring at her, a knowing half smile on his lips.

She let go of his hand and stepped back. "Okay." The word came out a little breathy and she forced herself to get a grip. "Now put that in the bowl and then flip on the mixer to beat it smooth for a minute. Then we'll add the next ingredient."

Eric did as she said, the smile still on his face. They

continued down the list of ingredients, Nat correcting him on nearly every ingredient until they had almost incorporated everything.

"Okay, all we have left is the flour mixture with all of our dry ingredients."

"I still don't see why we couldn't have just put them in without having to combine them all first. Doesn't it all just get mixed in together anyways?"

"Yes but it incorporates better if it's all sifted together before you put it in with the wet ingredients."

"Whatever." Eric shrugged and did as she directed. "All right, boss lady, what's next?"

"Grab the milk. We're going to alternate the flour mixture with the milk until everything is all mixed together."

Eric poured out the milk into the measuring cup and grabbed another cup to scoop up some of the flour mixture. Before Natalie could stop him, he dumped an overflowing cup of flour into the already beating mixer.

"Wait!" Nat said. But it was too late. Flour sprayed everywhere, covering them both. Eric, who had been bending over the mixer, stood up and turned toward her. His face was completely covered in flour. Natalie slapped her hand over her mouth but couldn't contain her laughter. He glared at her and ran a hand through his hair, sending more flour into the air.

Nat choked off her laugh. "When you're adding the flour, you need to turn the mixer off first."

"Oh really? Ya think? That probably would have been good to know before I put the flour in."

"Sorry. I just sort of assumed you'd know that already."

Eric snorted. "I think it's safe to assume that when it comes to baking, I know nothing."

"Ya think?" Nat said, mimicking him.

"Oh, this is funny, is it?"

Natalie's laughter bubbled over again. She really couldn't help it. But with him standing there, white from the eyebrows down, the flour mixing with whatever product he had in his hair to turn into a white paste, she just couldn't keep it in.

"I'm sorry, I really am. But, oh my God." She burst out laughing.

Eric walked toward her and Nat stepped back until she was up against the sink. He grinned with a predatory leer and took another step closer. She reached behind her and grabbed the sprayer, holding it out in front of her like a weapon.

"Don't come any closer!"

Eric froze for a second, then dodged to the side, laughing as he ducked around behind her. She sprayed the nozzle at him but only succeeded in misting them both with water before he got it out of her hands.

He reached out and grabbed her around the waist, hauling her into him. "*Hmmm*, is it still funny?" he asked, shaking his head over her and sending a shower of flour cascading down onto her head.

Nat shrieked and tried twisting away from him, but Eric laughed, holding her even tighter as he rubbed himself all over her. By the time he stopped they were both covered in flour and breathless with laughter.

Nat looked up. Eric's mouth was mere inches from hers. His arms were still firmly around her, his body pressed against hers. She leaned in a little and hesitated while her mind warred with itself. *This is a bad, bad idea.* But it would be so easy to close the distance between them. So easy. And so good. She leaned a fraction of an inch closer and Eric took the decision out of her hands.

He slipped a hand into her hair, cupping the back of her head to bring her closer. His lips closed over hers and Nat didn't even pretend to fight it. She wrapped her arms around his neck, opening her mouth to bring him in even deeper. Eric groaned and crushed her to him, lifting her to the counter.

Nat wrapped her legs around his waist, drawing him in as close as he could get. He slipped his fingers under her shirt, brushing against her skin in featherlight touches that had her shivering against him. He trailed up her rib cage to just beneath her bra. When his thumbs brushed over her nipples, she gasped and arched into him, pressing into his hands. He fumbled with the clasp of her bra and she reached up and quickly unhooked it, laughing a bit as she yanked it out through the sleeve of her shirt and tossed it to the side.

Her hands tugged on Eric's shirt and he whipped it over his head. Hers followed and then there was nothing between them. Nothing but his mouth on her skin, his tongue drawing her nipple into the scalding heat of his mouth. Nat struggled to catch her breath, her hands threading through his hair, grabbing handfuls as she held on for dear life.

Eric's straining jeans pressed against the thin material of her yoga pants, fitting perfectly against her. Nat's legs clenched, her hips lifting to rub against the hard length of him. Eric pressed against her again and again. Once more and Nat cried out, throwing her head back as her release shuddered through her body. Eric held her, relinquishing her nipple to explore her mouth. He let the wave of her orgasm ride through her before he pressed against her again, searching for his own release.

Nat slipped a hand between them and massaged him through his jeans. She tore her mouth from his and kissed her way down his neck, across his chest, her teeth lightly grazing one nipple. Eric sucked in a breath and grabbed a fistful of her hair. He pulled her head back up and crushed his mouth to hers, his tongue mimicking the movement of his hips as he thrust against her. Nat's hand rubbed and squeezed as she rocked against him until he stiffened, thrust again, once more, and then relaxed against her, sucking in great gulps of air.

They clung to each other for a moment, their hearts pounding together. Nat let her head rest against Eric's chest for a second while she caught her breath. When she finally thought she could speak, she lifted her head and looked up at Eric. He smiled down at her.

"That was…" He laughed. "I have no words."

"Ditto," Nat said.

Eric leaned down to kiss her, his hand cupping her cheek, one thumb gently rubbing against her face as his lips moved over hers. The aftershocks of her orgasm still faintly pulsed through her but Nat could feel the heat building again.

A faint sound from across the room snapped her out of the haze of pleasure Eric's lips were creating.

"What's that?" Nat asked, wrenching her mouth from Eric's.

"What?" he murmured, his lips trailing down her throat.

"That!" Nat said, hearing a distinct murmur of voices from the direction of the door. She pushed on Eric a bit, finally getting his attention.

This time he heard it too. He disentangled himself from her, snagging their shirts from the floor and helping her jump off the counter. They were both still covered in flour. Nothing much they could do about that. At least it was explainable. The voices were louder. Gina and Jared, arguing as usual.

Nat and Eric did a quick perusal of each other and gave each other a thumbs up. Nat's legs were still quivering, and her body felt like a puddle of melted frosting, but that didn't account for the oddly free feeling she had.

"Shit!" she gasped, grabbing her breasts in both hands. Her totally free and unencumbered breasts. Where the hell was her bra? Eric saw her dilemma and they both turned to search for it.

"Do you smell that?" Eric asked.

"That burning smell?"

"Yeah."

"Oh my God!" Nat lunged for the mixer that had been forgotten during their impromptu make-out session. The paddle was still spinning, creaming the batter into oblivion. Somehow her bra had gotten tangled up with the paddle handle and the motor was working overtime to keep mixing.

Eric yanked the power cord from the wall and worked furiously to untangle the bra from the machine. "Got it!" he said, holding the scrap of cloth up in triumph.

The kitchen door clicked open. Eric's eyes went from the door, to Nat, to the bra in his hand. Before Nat could say a word, he stretched it in his hands like a rubber band and slingshot it to the top of the fridge. It disappeared almost entirely, only one of the satiny straps hanging off the side.

Nat stared with her mouth hanging open but had no chance to say or do anything before Jared and Gina burst in.

"You're a fungus," Gina said, glaring at Jared in disgust.

"*Hmm*, like a mushroom? Earthy and delicious, maybe a little mind-altering? I can dig that. You wanna taste?"

"*Ugh*," Gina groaned. "Eric, you better check your boy here or he's going to get his junk punched."

"Hey, don't blame him on me. I've got no control over him. You're the one walking in with him."

"Yeah, not my fault. Ran into him at Starbucks and the miscreant followed me all the way over here."

"Hey, I was at Starbucks first. I can't help it if you're stalking me. I just figured I'd save you the trouble of following me and escort you over. We were both headed here, anyway."

"Right. Whatever."

Gina's eyes narrowed as she looked back and forth between Eric and Nat and the flour-covered kitchen. "What the hell happened here?"

"Just a little baking accident," Nat said.

"She was showing me how to make cupcakes," Eric

chimed in. "I'm not a very good student."

Gina looked him up and down, her eyes narrowing as her gaze zoomed in on his crotch. "Uh-huh. Looks like Nat was being a very thorough teacher."

Nat frowned slightly, trying to catch Gina's meaning. Then she followed Gina's gaze and nearly swallowed her tongue. Embarrassed heat immediately shot to her cheeks, burning so hotly she thought she'd melt on the spot. Eric frowned at her, trying to figure out what was going on. Nat's eyes dropped to his crotch, then back up. He looked down. And immediately turned his back, his hands brushing at what was very obviously the flour imprint of a hand.

Gina looked like she couldn't decide if she wanted to yell at them or laugh her ass off. Though laughing was definitely winning out. "I just stopped by to see if you wanted to start on refinishing the display case. But…" Her gaze bounced from Eric to Nat and back again. "I guess we can just get started on that without you, for now. We'll just, um, let you guys get cleaned up a bit," she said, grabbing Jared's arm and towing him out the door.

"What's going on? Did I miss something?" Jared asked.

"Always. Just keep walking."

Jared didn't bother arguing, just launched back into another attempt on Gina's virtue. "Ah, if you wanted to get me alone, all you had to do was ask. I'd follow you anywhere, baby."

"I swear, if you say one more thing…"

Their voices trailed off and Nat slumped against the counter, a nervous laugh escaping, along with a sigh of relief.

Eric grabbed a damp towel and scrubbed at his jeans. "So. I'm thinking black jeans are a really bad idea for the kitchen."

Nat laughed and Eric reached a hand out. She hesitated a second, feeling suddenly shy, but let him take her hand. He pulled her to him and gave her a gentle kiss. "I know I should apologize for totally mauling you in the middle of the kitchen but…that was just…"

"I know," Nat agreed, her lips stretching into a slow smile she couldn't stop if she wanted to.

"Fucking amazing."

Her smile spread wider. "Took the words right out of my mouth."

Eric chuckled, a low, deep sound full of primal male pride. He had a right to be proud. Not that full-on sex with him hadn't been completely mind-blowing, but there was a lot to be said for a good old-fashioned make-out fest.

"How about we get cleaned up and go grab something to eat," he said.

"Okay. Just one thing."

"Anything you want," Eric said, pulling her close for another kiss.

"Can you get my bra down?"

Eric burst out laughing. "Yeah, sorry. Couldn't think what else to do with it."

He went to the fridge and pulled it down. "Hey, how about we go on a real date?"

Natalie froze. "A date?"

"Yeah. You know, one of those things where I come pick you up. We go somewhere together, maybe have dinner and then a movie or something so we can sit in the dark and hold hands," he said with a wink and a grin.

Nothing had ever sounded so wonderful. But… "I don't know if we should."

Eric wrapped his arms around her waist and pulled her in for a kiss. "Oh yeah," he said, cupping her face. "We definitely should. I know you wanted to take it slow, but we've seen each other every day now for almost two months. I've spent more time with you than I have with Jared, and I live with him."

Nat smiled, wavering. He was right. Honestly, she felt like

she knew him better than most people in her life. And she wanted to get to know him a whole lot better. She wanted to date him. Wanted to spend time outside of the bakery with him. And she was tired of wanting it. No, their business matters weren't worked out just yet, but their personal situation seemed far more urgent.

His lips descended, moving over hers until her head started swimming and she had to clutch his shoulders to keep from swaying. "You're playing dirty," she murmured.

"Man's gotta do what a man's gotta do." His lips went back to their diversionary tactics.

She grinned. "All right, fine. Let's go out."

"Good." He kissed the tip of her nose. "Don't worry about this mess. We can deal with it later. Go get cleaned up. I'll meet you at your place in an hour."

One last kiss and he was out the door before Nat could say anything else. She prayed she wasn't making a huge mistake. The bakery would be up and running soon and then what? He wouldn't need her anymore. The men in her life didn't tend to stick around very long after she was no longer useful. And she really didn't think she could go through that all again. Though, Eric didn't seem like the type to just ditch her. But then, neither had Steve.

Mistake or not, she was about to go on her first real date with her Gelato man. And she was grinning like an idiot.

Heaven help her.

# Chapter Fourteen

If he hadn't already thought she was damn near the perfect woman before, he did now. She'd not only sat through a showing of *Die Hard* without giving him a hard time, but she'd actually enjoyed it, as far as he could tell. He was half tempted to drop to one knee and propose right there. A thought that shocked him to his core when he realized he meant it.

He shook off the unsettling thought. Nat was skittish enough as it was. If he declared his interest in making their relationship an actual relationship, let alone a permanent one, they'd be back to being "just friends" faster than he could say *yippee ki-yay, mother fu—*

"Does the theater do this often?" Nat asked. "Do old movie marathons?"

"About once a month. Last month was a *Lethal Weapon* marathon."

"Fun." Nat grinned.

"So, you're a *Die Hard* fan, huh?"

Nat shrugged and took a sip of her soda, chewing on the straw a bit. "What's not to like? It's got action, humor. And a hot, young Bruce Willis."

Eric grinned.

"What?" Nat asked.

"Nothing." He reached down and threaded his fingers through hers.

She glanced down at their hands and smiled, giving his hand a slight squeeze as they started walking off.

When they passed the bathroom, she let go, dropping her cup into a nearby trash can. "I'm going to pop in real quick," she said, nodding at the restroom.

"I'll wait out here. Want me to hold your purse for you?"

She laughed softly and handed him her bag. "Sure. Be right back." She disappeared into the crowd of women streaming in and out of the doors, leaving him holding the black bag he'd only sort of jokingly offered to hold.

Eric leaned against the wall and spent a few minutes wondering about the possibility of getting her back to his place again. Probably slim to none. Then again, she did seem…

He froze, his thoughts coming to a screeching halt. If there was a God, Eric's immobility would render him invisible and the last person in the world he wanted to see would keep right on walking.

No such luck. Courtney sashayed out of the bathroom and made a beeline right for him.

"Well, Eric Schneider. We seem to keep running into each other, don't we?"

Eric inwardly groaned and debated how badly his mother would yell at him if he were to run in the other direction and pretend he hadn't seen Courtney. He'd probably be disowned on the spot. Which might not be an altogether bad thing. It would be nice to not have to worry about keeping the peace by being social with girls like Courtney.

"Here by yourself?" she asked, sidling up to him.

He glanced down at the purse in his hands. "Yeah, all

alone."

She smirked. "Well, if you need a date for the night…" she said, ignoring his pointed look.

"Maybe another time."

Courtney pouted but didn't take the hint. "So, what did you see?"

Eric plastered a fake smile on his face, his one defense mechanism against social butterflies like Courtney and her crowd. "*Die Hard.*"

"*Ugh.* You always did like those action films. Why waste time and money seeing a movie you've already seen a hundred times?" He smiled at her, knowing it probably looked more like a grimace than anything else. He also knew Courtney wouldn't even notice. Thankfully, her gaggle of friends came out of the bathroom in one huge swarm.

"You know, I'm actually glad I ran into you. I'm really not feeling well and my friends are going to a party. Would you mind driving me home?"

"Oh, well…" He turned to find Natalie waiting for him near the bathroom door.

"I wouldn't ask, but I really don't feel up to walking right now," she said, her lips puckered into a little pout. She pressed her hand against her belly for good measure.

Eric was 99 percent sure Courtney was feeding him a total line of bullshit, but she did look a little pale. Though with her, it was hard to tell. She was always pale. However, if he refused and found out later she really had been sick he'd feel like shit. Even worse, if he refused and she told his mother, his life would be hell for weeks. Easier to just drive her home and get it over with.

Nat joined them, her forehead creased in a slight frown as she looked back and forth between them. He looked apologetically at her. "Nat, Courtney isn't feeling well. Do you mind if we drop her at home?"

Her frown deepened for a moment but then she turned to Courtney with a faint smile. "Of course. We can't just abandon her, can we?"

Eric turned for the door, not believing for a moment that Nat was okay with this, but grateful all the same that she wasn't making a big deal about it. The woman was a saint.

Courtney babbled non-stop, sounding less and less ill by the second, until they reached Eric's car. Eric opened the passenger door for Nat but Courtney butted her way in.

"Do you mind if I sit in front? I get carsick when I sit in the back and since I'm already not feeling well…" She pulled the pout and belly rub again and it was all Eric could do not to roll his eyes right in her face.

Nat gave Courtney that smile that didn't reach her eyes again. "Of course not. We wouldn't want you to be uncomfortable."

Courtney slid into the front seat, aiming what she probably thought was a sweet smile at Eric. He gritted his teeth and closed the door. Nat didn't wait for him to open her door and she damn near slammed it on his hand when he tried to close it for her. He couldn't even be pissed at her. Frankly, he was counting his lucky stars she hadn't kneed him in the balls yet. He was pretty sure he deserved it. My God, he was ready to hold himself down and *let* her do it. Their first date and she was relegated to the backseat so he could chauffeur Courtney home.

Courtney chattered the entire way to her atrocity of an industrial loft. Eric ignored her, his gaze meeting Nat's in the rearview mirror every few seconds. The first time, her glare was enough to make him tuck his tender bits between his legs and scurry into hiding.

The more Courtney babbled on though, the more Nat's expression lightened. Eric waggled his eyebrows at Nat and her lips even pulled into a tiny smile, which she literally bit off, her teeth clamping onto her bottom lip. The sight hit him like a fist in the gut. What he wouldn't give to be able to nibble on that lip himself. As soon as he got rid of the obnoxious third wheel riding shotgun.

When he pulled up to the curb, Courtney sat and fiddled with her skirt, obviously waiting for him to do the gentlemanly thing. He repressed a sigh and got out to open her door. Nat got out along with her.

"It was nice talking to you earlier," Courtney said to Nat.

Eric frowned. When had they spoken? She reached up and kissed his cheek and Eric barely resisted the urge to shove her away. He politely waited until the doorman had let her in, then turned around with a groan. He really needed to have a talk with his mother about constantly foisting Courtney on him. They both needed to get it through their heads he wasn't remotely interested in her.

The girl he was interested in was already ensconced back in his car. Though she'd moved to the front seat, so that was something at least.

"Sorry about that," he murmured when he got back in.

Nat shrugged. "You couldn't just abandon her to walk home when she was so sick."

Eric would bet his left ball sack she was laying the sarcasm on thick but she said it with such a sickly sweet tone of voice, he really wasn't sure.

"Yeah. Well, thanks for being cool with it."

"No problem," she said quietly before turning her attention to the view out her window.

They drove in silence for a few minutes. He wasn't sure what she wanted to do, but they weren't too far from his place so when he passed an open parking spot he pulled in. Nat got out before he could say anything.

She slung her bag over her shoulder and shoved her hands into her pockets, hunching her shoulders a little. He wondered if her hands were just cold or if she was trying to avoid holding his hand again. They started walking in the direction of Nat's building. Not the direction Eric wanted to go. The closer they got to her apartment, the less he wanted to say good night.

"So, do you want to go grab some coffee or something?" he asked.

"It's actually getting a little late. And we've got the market sale to get ready for."

"Market?" Eric asked, fighting back his disappointment. The night had been going so well. "I thought that wasn't for two more days."

Nat smiled, shaking her head. "It's not. But you can't whip up enough desserts to sell in one morning. We need to decide what we want to make, get prepped, make some signage, get tables and everything ready, make sure your business cards are picked up and ready to go. Plus those brochures we were going to do. Not to mention actually making everything. That takes a few days."

"If you say so."

She rolled her eyes and Eric smiled. Needling her was one of the best parts of his day. He loved watching the sparks fly when he got under her skin.

"Yes, I say so."

"Well, you're the boss lady, Cupcake."

Nat chuckled. "Stop calling me that."

"What else should I call you?"

"You could call me by my name."

"Yeah. I could. But it wouldn't be as fun."

She snorted. They'd reached her apartment. "Well."

"Well." He stepped closer and she looked down at her feet. He ran his hands up and down her arms and pulled her to him.

"Eric," she said, putting her hand on his chest. "We

shouldn't."

"Yes. We should." He leaned down and captured her lips. Just that slight touch and he instantly craved more. He'd never get enough of her.

She made a little noise deep in her throat that hit him right in the gut. He pulled her against him, wrapping his arms about her so he could deepen the kiss.

"*Ugh*! Get a room."

Nat jerked out of his arms and he turned to glare at Gina.

"Don't give me that look. Some of us are trying to get into their apartments."

Eric opened his mouth to say something but Nat drew farther away from him, stepping up onto the stairs.

"We were…just saying good night."

"Uh-huh. None of my business. Carry on, if you must." Gina trotted up the stairs and pulled out her keys.

"No, it's okay. It's getting late. Hold the door," she called to Gina.

Eric frowned at her. What the hell was happening?

Nat turned back to him. "I'll, um, see you tomorrow, okay?"

"Hey," he said, reaching for her hand. She hesitated, but finally took his hand. "Everything okay?"

"Yeah. Fine. I'm tired. For the past couple of weeks I've had to get up at the crack of dawn to bake the cupcakes and help Gina get the truck ready. It's been a long month."

"Yeah. I guess it has." He tugged her forward a little and pressed a gentle kiss to her cheek. "I'll see you in the morning then."

"Okay. Thanks for dinner. And the movie."

"It was my pleasure." Or was almost his pleasure anyway. No thanks to Gina. "Good night, Cupcake."

She gave him a slight smile. "Good night, Gelato." She jogged up the rest of the stairs and went inside.

Eric waited until the door had closed behind her and then pulled out his phone and texted Jared to see where he was. A few moments later Jared texted back. He was at the bar near their building. Fifteen minutes later he was sitting next to Jared on a bar stool, nursing a cold beer.

"I don't know why you're so upset, man. Didn't sound like anything happened."

"How would you feel if you went on a date with some girl and some other guy pushed his way in, conned his way into a ride home during which you had to sit in the back, and then hung all over her when he got out? I'm amazed she's still talking to me."

"So maybe she really does like you and is willing to overlook a little jealousy to keep seeing you." Jared finished his beer and slapped Eric on the back. "You let me know if you figure it out."

Eric nodded vaguely in Jared's direction. Did Nat actually like him enough to be jealous?

God, he hoped so. But he definitely needed to set her straight about Courtney. He wasn't going to lie; it was a little flattering that she was jealous. But it so wasn't worth ruining what he was trying to build with her. The woman was stubborn enough as it was. The last thing he needed was another obstacle.

Time for a little damage control.

# Chapter Fifteen

Controlling whatever damage Courtney had caused turned out to be more difficult than Eric thought. Nat seemed to be her normal self, yet she'd somehow managed to avoid being alone with him for two days. Any time he made any move to touch her she found an excuse to move away. It was so subtle it had taken him half the day to realize what she was doing. Like when he'd put his hand on her arm and she'd dropped a spoon and bent to retrieve it. Or when he'd put his hand on her back and she turned away to sneeze. Nothing he could really pinpoint as her purposely trying to keep his hands off her. But there was definitely something up.

By lunch on the second day, Eric was fed up. He cornered Nat in the cooler. She turned around, holding a box of butter in each hand like she was going to clobber him at the slightest provocation.

"Eric. What are you doing?" Her voice was wary and a bit annoyed. Good. She wasn't the only one.

"What's going on, Nat?"

She lowered the boxes and tried to push past him. "I don't

know what you mean."

He stuck an arm out. "Yes. You do."

She stepped to the other side but he countered her move. "I thought we had a great time the other night. We had fun at the movies. And a hell of a lot of fun before the movies." He took a step closer and she dropped her gaze, refusing to meet his eyes. He gently took her chin in his fingers and lifted her face. "What's going on, Nat?" he asked again.

"Can we get out of here, please. I'm freezing."

Eric took a couple steps backward, far enough that they were out of the freezer, but not so far that she could make her escape. She sighed and glared at him.

"Nothing is going on, Eric. We've got work to do. The farmer's market is tomorrow and we need to get everything ready if you want to do a sneak peek for the bakery."

"Screw the market."

Nat's eyes widened, her mouth dropping open in a little O. God, she was cute when she was pissed.

"Screw the market? We've been working for weeks to get this damn bakery ready and the market is the perfect opportunity to introduce you to the neighborhood. You can't just say 'screw the market.' I thought you wanted this bakery to succeed."

"What I want," he said, stepping even closer, "is for you to tell me what happened after the movies. Because all I know is that we were having a great time and ever since then, you've hardly spoken two words to me. Nothing that's not bakery related. And if I try and touch you"—he ran his hand down her arm and she flinched—"you do that."

Nat crossed her arms over her chest. "It's not a big deal, Eric. I know that we were just messing around. And I know about your little girlfriend. So, let's just forget anything happened between us and get back to work, okay?"

Eric frowned, racking his brain for anything that might

have given her the idea that he had a girlfriend. "Nat…what the hell are you talking about?"

She glared at him. "Oh, just drop it already, Eric."

"No. I'm not dropping this. I was not, ever, just screwing around with you." He lightly gripped her upper arms, ready to let go if she fought him at all, but wanting desperately to hold her against him. "And I do not have a girlfriend. Where did you get that idea?"

"From your girlfriend," she said, yanking out of his grasp. "Courtney Collins. The 'special friend' you had to pick up from the airport. And take home from the movies. And give financial advice to, I'm betting. And escort to a birthday party. The one that is always hanging all over you."

"Courtney?" He gritted his teeth against the urge to find Courtney and shake her until she got it through her thick head they were *never* going to be together.

"Yes, Courtney. She was in the bathroom at the movies. Told me all about you two. Growing up together, dating all through high school. How much your parents can't wait for your engagement announcement that she's certain is coming any day now. And how frustrating it is for her that you still feel the need to sow a few wild oats and how she'd be ever so much obliged if I'd quit helping you in that department."

"She said *what*?" Eric was going to throttle Courtney next time he saw her. How dare she? He knew the spoiled brat was used to getting her way but he'd had no clue the lengths she'd go to get it.

Nat walked over to the counter and put the butter down. "It's not a big deal. We had a little fun, but I am not really a wild oats kind of girl. So, let's just focus on getting your bakery off the ground and then we can go our separate ways, okay?"

Those words struck Eric like a sucker punch in the gut. *Oh, hell no.* He was *not* losing her that easily.

"No, it's not okay."

He reached her in two steps, grabbed her face, his hands threading through her hair, and pulled her to him. She didn't resist when their lips met, not for a moment. He crushed her to him, wanting to show her how much she meant to him with a desperation that startled him.

She kissed him back. Her lips moved under his, opened to him, drew him in. For a few sweet seconds, she met his passion with her own. Then she wrenched her mouth from his with a strangled whisper. "Stop."

He stopped. But he kept his arms around her, pressed his forehead to hers.

"Nat, listen to me very carefully. Courtney is *not* my girlfriend."

Nat jerked in his arms, but he didn't let go and she stopped fighting him.

"Yes, we dated in high school, for six months. But she was, and still is, a spoiled brat that I can't stand to be around for longer than two seconds. Yes, my parents probably would love it if we announced our engagement, but that is one of the many, many things my parents and I disagree on. Yes, they force her company on me whenever they possibly can, and most of the time it's easier to give in and babysit her for a few hours than deal with them. But she and I… It's never going to happen. And I've told Courtney that, in no uncertain terms, at least a hundred times. Apparently, she still hasn't gotten the message."

He tilted Nat's face up so her gaze was forced to meet his. "I don't know what we have between us, Nat. I don't know where it's going or even where I want it to go. But I swear to you, this is not just some game to me. I am not just messing around with you. You are not my wild oat. You are my Cupcake," he said with a little grin.

Nat stared at him for a second and then laughed a little, shaking her head. "What the hell does that mean?"

"I have no fucking clue," he said, laughing with her. "Maybe it just means you're mine." He smiled at her, his heart skipping a little when she finally smiled back. "What do you mean when you call me Gelato?"

Her cheeks flushed a little and it was all Eric could do to keep from pressing her against the wall and kissing her until she begged him for more. Damn, but the woman was adorable when she blushed.

"Maybe it just means you are sweet and delicious and addicting…even if I know you're bad for me."

Eric slowly nodded. "Maybe." He reached out and gently stroked a thumb over her cheek. "Then again, just because something is sweet doesn't mean it's bad for you. Maybe we just need to learn to balance it with everything else in our lives."

Nat looked up and gave him a small smile. "Maybe."

"But we'll never figure it out if you keep pushing me away."

Nat sighed. "Eric, I'm not sure I'm ready…"

"I'm not asking for a huge commitment, Nat. I'm just asking…that you give us a chance. Let's go out a few more times. See if we like each other. For more than the obvious," he said, rubbing his thumb along her lower lip.

Her breath kicked up a notch and she turned slightly, pressing her face into his hand, gazing up at him from under her lashes.

Eric's own breath grew ragged, heat searing through him from where her breath burned hot against his skin straight to his groin, which was beginning to ache for attention.

"Well, I know how I feel about you in that department, but I wasn't sure if you felt the same way," she said, her voice low and husky and oddly uncertain.

"God, how can you even doubt it?"

Nat bit her lip with a little shrug and it was all he could do not to toss her up on the counter and take her right there, show her how well suited they were, in *all* departments. He closed his eyes and dropped his hand, his mind furiously struggling for any image that might erase the thought of her, legs spread wide in invitation, with that incredibly sexy smile on her lips.

*Grandma. Uncle Joe in his Speedos. Jared picking his teeth with a fork.*

He took a tremulous breath and opened his eyes to find her watching him, a growing smile on her lips.

"If we didn't have to work…" he said, his tone both warning and promising.

"But we do," she said, her grin widening as she pulled away.

He couldn't let her go just yet. Not until he knew for sure they were good.

"Nat, are we…?"

"Yeah. We're good."

He drew her close and kissed her, his blood surging when she rose on her toes to kiss him back.

"Mamma Mia" started playing from his pocket.

Nat pulled away from him, laughing. "Seriously?"

Eric groaned and silenced his phone, then tried to bring her back into his arms.

She playfully pushed him away. "All right, enough of that nonsense. We've got work to do or we'll never be ready for tomorrow."

"Yes, boss lady."

Nat smiled that sweet smile of hers that made all other thoughts evaporate from his mind and then she turned back to whatever she'd been going to make. When her attention was caught by the rolling rack of pastries they had ready for the next day, she froze, and Eric braced himself for another battle.

"Eric. What are these?" Nat stared at a rack full of honey-laden baklava.

"Okay, hear me out."

"I thought you agreed that serving a Greek dish in an Italian bakery—"

"Yeah, I know. Not good for branding. But come on! It's so good. I grew up watching my aunt make this stuff. It's my absolute favorite."

She folded her arms and cocked an eyebrow. "You made all this on your own?"

"Yes."

"When."

"Last night."

The eyebrow rose higher.

"Well, I was bored and couldn't sleep and you weren't returning my phone calls so…"

She at least had the grace to blush at that.

"Just taste it."

Before she could protest, he snagged a piece and popped it in her mouth. She batted his hand away, covering her mouth while she chewed. He licked the honey from his fingers, watching her face for any sign of enjoyment. Or disgust.

Her eyes widened.

*That's a good sign, isn't it?*

Then her mouth puckered. Not a good sign. She quickly spun and headed for the sink. It took her a good minute and a half to get it all out of her mouth. *Bad sign. Really bad sign.*

"Damn," he said, "I thought I had that batch."

She gulped down a glass of water. "Well…the first layer wasn't bad, so that's an improvement. But the middle layers were like some sort of toasted tar. Like you somehow managed to both burn and undercook them simultaneously. That takes serious talent."

He scowled at her. "I'll get it right, eventually."

She didn't look convinced.

"Look, I understand that you don't think it should be on

the menu, but it's my favorite dessert and I want to give it a shot. So, here's my suggestion. Since the reason we are going to the market is to give the neighborhood a taste of what we'll be offering, as you say, let me take the baklava—or, you know, a few good batches that you'll have to help with—and we can see how it goes. If people start stumbling around in confusion at the utter audacity of an Italian bakery, that's not run by an Italian, daring to serve a Greek dessert, I'll toss the baklava and never mention it again. Scout's honor."

"Uh-huh. Were you even a scout?"

"I was actually. Eagle scout."

Her eyes widened again. *Ha! Got her there.*

"But," he continued, "if it does well and people like it, as I know they will, I'll put it on the menu. Deal?" He held out his hand.

A corner of her mouth quirked up. "Fine, deal." She took his hand and shook it, not resisting when he towed her closer.

"What are you doing?" she asked.

"Just helping you. You've got a little honey…" He leaned down and kissed her, sucking at the sticky spot on her lip. "Right there." He kissed her again.

She leaned into him, slipping her arms around his waist. But before they could get too far into their make-up make out, the front door to the bakery opened and Gina and Jared came barreling in. Nat stepped away from him and turned to busy herself at the counter.

"All right," Jared said, rubbing his hands together. "Your lovely baking assistants are here."

Gina rolled her eyes but grabbed an apron and put it on. "Point me where you need me," she said.

Eric wished he could grab Nat and whisk her off to his apartment to show her just how much he'd been missing her the last few days. But they had a shit-ton of pastries to bake. Time to get to it.

# Chapter Sixteen

By noon the next day, they only had one tray of baklava left and Nat was forced to admit they had been a smashing success. While several customers thought it an interesting item to have on the menu, none of them seemed to care in the least. They found it much more hilarious to be served Italian pastries from a place called Tuscan Treats by a six-foot-four blond-haired obvious descendant of Vikings. But no doubts about it, Tuscan Treats was off to an amazing start.

They'd already given out nearly all the brochures they'd brought, handed out dozens of cards, and set up appointments for three catering consultations. Better yet, they were selling the pastries they'd brought, and even the baklava, faster than they could put them out. At the rate they were going, they'd be out of things to sell before the market closed at two o'clock.

Even better was watching Eric as he interacted with his customers. He'd been a little hesitant at first, wanting to hang back and supervise instead of actually being a part of the sales. But Nat wasn't having any of that. If he wanted to run this bakery, then he needed to be more than the head honcho in the back. He needed to be a part of the whole process.

As the morning wore on, Eric got more and more into it. The more the customers complimented the pastries, the more excited they were over the opening of the bakery, the more Nat could see his pride shining through.

Eric finished boxing up a dozen cannoli for his customer and came to stand beside Nat.

"It's going well," he said, his smile stretching from ear to ear.

Nat had never seen him look so happy. "It *is* going very well. You should be very proud. You've really built something amazing, I think."

"*We've* built something amazing," he said, nudging her with his elbow. "None of this would be remotely possible without you."

Nat's cheeks burned, but she was pleased. "I don't know. You are very determined. I'm sure you would have found some way to make this work."

Eric laughed. "Maybe. But having you on board has made my life…"

He paused and looked at her in a way that made her knees go weak. *Good God, does the man know what kind of effect he has on me?*

"Better," he finished, reaching out to brush a thumb across her cheek. "Nat, I…"

Nat gasped and froze, her body running hot and cold in such quick succession her head spun. Because walking toward her, his arm around a woman Nat had thought was his assistant, was her ex-fiancé Steve. Nat would have been very, *very* happy to have never seen the cheating bastard again. And she certainly didn't want to see him when she'd been standing out in the sun and wind all morning. Yes, she hated him, but she was vain enough to want him to think she looked good.

"Nat?" Eric asked.

"Shit, he's coming this way." Nat looked around, wondering if Steve had seen her yet. *Can I duck under the table?* She could probably hide behind the boxes. No, that wouldn't work.

"Who's coming?" Eric asked, thoroughly confused.

Nat opened her mouth to answer but Steve turned in their direction and Nat jumped behind Eric. Not the ideal hiding spot maybe, but he was by far the biggest thing around. She put her hands on his waist, squeezing to keep him in place, and leaned her forehead on his back.

"Natalie?"

She apparently hadn't ducked fast enough. She took a deep breath and came out from behind a frowning Eric.

"Steve. Hi." She turned and looked up at Eric, patting his hip. "There, got that apron tied for you. Just had to get the knot out."

"Um, thanks." Eric was looking back and forth between Nat and Steve, his frown deepening.

"I thought I saw you back there," Steve said, a smile on his thin lips that didn't quite reach his eyes. "It's good to see you again."

Nat nodded, hoping the smile she plastered on her face wasn't as stiff as it felt. "It's good to see you, too." Her gaze flicked to the smirking woman on his arm. The one sporting a massive diamond that looked distinctly familiar. Nat swallowed back the bile that rose in her throat and acted like nothing was bothering her. "How are you?"

"Wonderful." His grin grew wider, though it still didn't touch the cold depth of his eyes. "Work at the restaurant is busier than ever, amazing reviews pouring in. We're booked solid for the next two months."

"That's great," she said, praying her voice held steady. Nat couldn't keep from glancing at the woman again, Phoebe, she believed her name was. Especially since good old Pheebs was draping her hand over Steve's arm in just the right way for her diamonds to catch the light and shine right on Nat's face.

Steve noticed Nat's glance and nodded at his companion. "You remember Phoebe?"

"Yes, of course. Good to see you again. Nice ring," she said, unable to resist mentioning it.

"Thanks," Phoebe purred. "It was Steve's grandmother's. She was so excited when we got engaged, she insisted I have it."

"Really?" Nat's blood was beginning to boil. All the rage she'd thought she'd gotten over after Steve had run out on her a month before their wedding was flooding back. Bringing with it an overwhelming urge to curl into the fetal position and cry her heart out. Which just pissed her off even more. She hadn't planned on saying anything, but screw it.

"He told me it had been his mother's when he gave it to me. Though it looks much better on your finger than it did on mine. It takes a good solid finger to pull off that look. My fingers are much too slender. It just looked gaudy on me."

Phoebe stiffened, her eyes narrowing dangerously. But Nat was amused to see Steve was getting as much of the glare as she was. Old Pheebs hadn't known that the ring had been Nat's first. Nat resisted the urge to smile.

"So," Steve said, his voice full of ice. "How's your little business going? I think I heard somewhere that you're doing something with cupcakes? Driving a...food truck, is it? Or no, a *cupcake truck,* I suppose."

Somehow he managed to pack a whole encyclopedia's worth of disdain in those two little words. Nat straightened, her hand knotting in her apron. That insufferable bastard!

"Though, maybe I was mistaken," Steve continued, his gaze taking in the table in front of them. "Did that not work out?"

Her arm brushed against Eric and she looked up into his concerned face. He'd moved closer to her during her little exchange with Steve, standing with his arms folded and just a hair in front of her like some sort of bodyguard.

"Actually," Eric said, his voice even colder than Steve's, "Nat owns the most successful mobile cupcakery in the city. In fact, she's been so successful that I hired her to set up my own bakery. I wanted to learn from the best."

"Ah," Steve said, his gaze clearing a bit. "So she works for you."

"No. She consults. At least that's how it started out," Eric said, slipping an arm around her waist and looking down at her with an adoring gaze. "But who could resist this gorgeous, amazing woman?"

He drew her in closer and kissed her on the forehead.

Nat didn't know what to do, or say. The part of her that wasn't still in shock over Steve and every insulting word out of his mouth was grateful for the part Eric was playing. But at the same time, the lie didn't sit right with her. Though...with the way Eric was looking at her, she couldn't tell it was a lie. And didn't *that* just curl her toes.

Steve cleared his throat and Nat realized she and Eric had been staring at each other like a couple of lovesick puppy dogs.

"Oh, sorry," Eric said, sounding anything but. "Well, it's been nice meeting you, Stan—"

"Steve," Steve said, glaring.

"But Nat and I need to get going. Our relief just got here and we've got somewhere to be."

Gina and Jared had indeed arrived, and if Steve knew what was good for him he'd get out of there before Gina jumped the table and raked him from neck to nuts with the hands she was already curling into claws. She was *not* a fan.

Steve seemed to have the same idea. "Well, it was good

seeing you again, Natalie." He took Phoebe's arm and nodded at Eric before pulling his pissed-off fiancée away from the Tuscan Treats booth.

Nat slumped against Eric. "Thank you. I'm sorry about that," she said, embarrassed almost to the point of tears that he had been there for the whole exchange, but incredibly grateful at the same time.

He kept his arm around her waist, squeezing her tight again while he yanked off his apron with one hand. "Gina, can you and Jared…?"

Gina grabbed the apron and nodded. "Yep, don't even worry about it. Take care of her."

Nat glanced at Gina, only vaguely realizing they were talking about her. She distantly understood she was moments away from losing her shit. Maybe getting away from all the nice market people would be a good idea.

Before she could gather enough wits about her to say something, Eric had gathered her up and was marching her away from the market toward the pub on the corner. Hot damn, at that moment she seriously loved the man. The pub was exactly what she needed. They had booze there. And chocolate. And booze. And didn't that just sound lovely? Anything that would wipe from her mind the image of the man she'd intended to spend her life with and the spectacular bitch who was wearing *her* ring.

Nat hated that the encounter was affecting her like this. Hated that Eric was seeing this weak side of her, the side she didn't show anyone, except Gina. But for the life of her, she couldn't rein it in. It had taken months after her breakup with Steve to pull herself back together and she'd obviously not gotten over him. Seeing him again, with that woman, hurt her on a level she hadn't even known was still possible. She didn't know why. She didn't love the man anymore. Never really had, she was realizing now. She hadn't felt a fraction of what she felt for Eric for Steve.

And didn't that thought just make her head spin? Forget it. Thinking hurt too much. She didn't want to do it anymore. She was going to go all Scarlett O'Hara and think about it tomorrow. Right now, she just wanted to make it all go away.

She prayed the pub had chocolate martinis.

# Chapter Seventeen

Eric watched as Nat downed her third chocolate martini. Maybe bringing her to a pub wasn't the best idea. Honestly, he'd just wanted to get some food in her, hoping that would help. She hadn't eaten all day and the pub was one of his favorite eating holes. They had the best pulled-pork sandwiches he'd ever eaten. And Nat wasn't really a drinker, from what he could tell. Other than sipping on some wine and the couple shots she'd done that one night at the club, he'd never seen her drink.

But now, it seemed like she wanted to make up for lost time. Not that he really blamed her. Adrenaline was still pumping through his system from the desire to pummel that massive asshole of an ex of hers. Eric was generally more the "kill them with laughter" type guy, but he'd be more than willing to make an exception in this case. He couldn't even imagine someone like Natalie with that shit bag.

Though seeing him explained a few things. Nat's commitment phobia, for instance. Not that they were at the commitment stage yet. But even getting the woman on a date had been harder than graduating from college. It was good to understand why. Partially. Because it also explained why Nat seemed so strangely reluctant to believe that Eric actually wanted her. Not just wanted to sleep with her but actually wanted *her*. If that oversize douche bag had dumped her for another woman, that helped explain why Nat didn't seem to realize how amazing she was. He was just going to have to try harder to prove it to her.

Nat waved the bartender over to order another drink but Eric shook his head. She turned and glared at him.

"Don't give me that look," he said. "I don't want to have to carry you out of here."

Nat shrugged and swiveled on her stool back toward the bar. Eric nudged her plate of food toward her. "Why don't you eat something? This is the best pork you've ever tasted, I promise."

Nat picked up a fry but used it to push the food around her plate. After a minute, she sighed and put it down. "I'm not really hungry right now. Can we just go home?"

Eric nodded. "Sure." He waved the waitress over and asked for some boxes for their uneaten food. He wiped his mouth and stood up. "I'm going to the restroom for just a second. You going to be okay?"

Nat snorted. "I think I can manage to be by myself for five minutes. I've managed fine so far."

Eric frowned and leaned down to kiss the top of her head. He hated the defeated sound in her voice. He'd never seen her like this. And he'd give anything to stop her from feeling like it now. Maybe he should let her have one more drink. She'd be hating life in the morning, but it wouldn't kill her and maybe a few hours of numbness would help. Plus, she didn't seem too bad off just yet. No slurring words and her eyes were clear. Too clear maybe. The pain was etched on her face like that asshole had freshly chiseled it.

He waved to the bartender and ordered her another chocolate martini. Nat glanced up at him with a surprised but grateful smile.

"Last one," he said. "But hell, who am I to stop you from getting shit-faced? I'd probably be doing it, too."

She gave him a wry smile and raised her newly filled glass in a salute. He smiled back and shook his head. "I'll be right back. Don't float away while I'm gone."

"No worries, Gelato," she said, taking a sip. "This is where they keep the booze. I'm not leaving."

Eric snorted and headed to the bathroom. He took care of business as fast as he could, not wanting to leave her alone longer than necessary. He was only gone five minutes. Tops. But apparently four martinis was her limit. Make that four martinis and a beer. Because unless the bartender had stopped by for a quick drink, Nat had downed his drink while he'd been gone. And she'd definitely taken on the flushed and glazed look of the inebriated.

He sighed and slapped down enough cash to cover their bill with a good tip and grabbed the bag the waitress had put their food in. "Come on," he said, helping Nat off the bar stool. "Let's get you home."

"Home. Yeah, home sounds good," she said, her words not nearly as clear as they'd been a few minutes earlier.

Eric helped her to his car, grateful he'd needed to bring it that morning to help haul baked goods. He slid in the driver's seat, pulling her over so her head was cradled on his shoulder.

"Sorry," she murmured.

"Don't worry about a thing," he said, holding her tighter, maneuvering through streets as fast as he could while still being safe as he drove one-handed.

She sniffed. "Great. Now I'm crying. *Ugh.*" She jerked off his shoulder and looked at him. "I'm not usually such a baby. It's just…it's just…"

Her face puckered and Eric's heart clenched, hating the pain he saw dulling her eyes.

"I know. It's okay. You don't have to be strong all the time."

"Yes, I do. He didn't think I'd amount to anything, you know. Said I'd never be good enough to make it on my own, without him. He didn't think I was capable of running my own business. Didn't think I was smart enough to help him run his. Nothing I did was ever good enough. I was just his back-up plan. The one he'd settle for if nothing better came along. But something did. So…out I went. I know I'm better off. But… still…"

Her head lolled back to his shoulder and she took a few deep, shuddering breaths. They pulled up outside her building and Eric thanked whatever higher power was on duty that day for the miracle of a parking spot right in front. He jumped out of the car and hurried around to help her out. He'd wanted to take her to his brownstone but figured she might be more comfortable with her own things.

She looked up at the building. "Hey." She grinned a little. "We're at my place."

Eric smiled at her. "Yep, we are. Do you have your keys?"

Nat nodded. "In my pocket."

Eric went fishing, trying to ignore the suggestive leer she aimed at him. "Hey now, you aren't getting frisky with me are you? 'Cause that'd be just fine with me. I think."

"Come on," Eric said, chuckling. "I'd love nothing more than to get frisky with you, but now's probably not a great time."

Nat thought about that while he fumbled with unlocking the door and holding her up at the same time.

"No," she said, hanging on him once he got the door open. "You're probably right. My head is a little fuzzy," she whisper-shouted.

"I bet," he said, helping her up the stairs. His house was looking better and better.

He finally got her up the stairs without too many more incidents. Once inside her apartment, he deposited her on the couch and went into the bathroom to run her a hot bath. He didn't know if it would help or not but his grandma had always said a hot bath cured anything, so it was worth a shot.

Eric found a little bottle of lavender bath oil, poured some of that in, and then went to get Nat. Helping her undress was an interesting procedure. He couldn't lie and say he didn't look. And yes, she was just as gorgeous as ever. But it surprised him a little that seeing her naked body only briefly inspired a few indecent thoughts. All of them filed away for later. Right now, he just wanted her to feel better. He wanted to erase that haunted, sad look on her face. Banish the sadness that darkened her eyes.

He helped her slip into the bath and then gently took out the elastic band that held her hair in a ponytail. She hugged her knees and closed her eyes as he began to wash her hair. Eric rubbed the vanilla-scented shampoo through her hair, letting the soapy strands slip through his fingers before washing out the suds. Then he rubbed some conditioner in, gently massaging her scalp. She sighed and tilted her head back into his hands.

"You know," she said, her voice barely audible. "It's not that I wish I was still with him. Or that I'm jealous that he's getting married. He bailed on me. Started canceling dates when other plans came up. I didn't know until too late that the other plans were *her*. I should have known. He only wanted me when there wasn't anyone better. I don't love him anymore. I don't want him. But…" Her voice cracked and tears leaked out from behind her closed eyes. "It hurts to know that he didn't love me, didn't want me."

Eric tenderly wiped away her tears and she turned her

face into his hand, opening her eyes to look at him. "He said he didn't want to get married. Ever. But obviously he didn't mean it. He just didn't want to marry *me*."

He didn't know what to say to make it better. Didn't know what to do. He kissed her forehead. "He's not good enough for you."

Eric made sure all the suds were out of her hair and helped her stand up and get out of the tub. He wrapped her hair up in one towel and grabbed another one to dry her off, before he wrapped her up in it.

"I don't want him," she insisted again, her voice sad and broken. "So why does it hurt so much to know he didn't want me? Why didn't he want me?"

Eric picked her up and cradled her in his arms. "Because he's an idiotic fool." He laid her gently on her bed and rummaged through her drawers until he found a comfy pair of cotton panties and a well-worn T-shirt that looked like she wore it as a nightgown. He helped slip her clothing on and then tucked her into bed.

"Stay with me?" she whispered.

"I'll be right here, I promise." He curled up behind her, wrapping his arms and legs around her so she was fully cocooned. She sighed and nuzzled back against him. He stroked her hair back from her face, keeping up the gentle caressing motions until her breathing deepened and she fell asleep.

He kissed her gently on the temple and let his eyes close, his heart beating in time to hers.

# Chapter Eighteen

Nat grabbed for the garbage can that had been placed conveniently next to the bed and vomited for the third time that morning. When she finished throwing up what she was sure was part of her intestine, she flopped back onto the bed, her hand pressing against her forehead in a useless attempt to keep her brain from pounding through her skull. At least it was dark in the room. Someone had thankfully drawn the curtains before the sun had crept in.

She rolled over, her head throbbing as she tried to remember the events of the night before. Vague memories of being bathed and carried and cradled like a baby stole through her aching head. She jerked up, immediately groaning at the pounding that spread from the tip of her head down to her quivering stomach. Nat curled back into the fetal position, trying to keep her body in one piece.

Eric. Eric had stayed with her all night. Had taken care of her, held her while she blubbered over that jackass Steve. Slept with his arms around her the whole night. A whole bundle of warm fuzzies filtered through her. He had been so unbelievably sweet it was almost more than she could stand. New tears threatened to escape, but she did her best to suck it up.

The door opened a crack and Eric peeked in. Seeing that she was awake, he slipped inside and sat beside her on the bed.

"Hey there," he said, his voice hardly more than a whisper. "How are you feeling?"

"Not great." She tried for a laugh but ended up gritting her teeth against an onslaught of nausea.

"Hang tight." Eric scooped up the trash can and carried it into the bathroom, ignoring Nat's protests to leave it there.

She could hear the water running in the tub as he rinsed it out. Nat knew she'd be completely mortified once she was back to her regular self. But all she could feel at the moment was a vague sense of embarrassment and overwhelming gratitude that she didn't have to haul her aching body out of bed just yet.

He came out of the bathroom a few minutes later and laid a cool washcloth on her forehead, setting the trash can on the floor where she could grab it if she needed it.

"Thank you," she said, taking his hand.

He smiled down at her. "My pleasure."

She snorted, grimacing when the sound and movement sent a fresh wave of pain through her head. "I seriously doubt that."

"No, I mean it. I don't mind at all. I'm glad I was here."

"Me too," she said, still holding on to his hand like he was her lifeline.

Their little business arrangement might be an unholy mess that needed straightening out, but Nat didn't give a damn about any of it at the moment.

"Why did you stay?" she asked.

He smiled again, brushing her hair out of her face as he

refolded the washcloth and placed the cool side against her heated skin. "Because you asked me to."

"You never do what I ask you to."

Eric chuckled. "I must have been feeling generous."

"I'm glad."

"Me too."

Eric leaned in but an ambush of *what the hell did I drink last night* hit her and Nat lurched to the side of the bed. Eric rubbed her back and held her hair while she heaved over the trash can. She finally sat back. He handed her a glass of water and she took it, rinsing her mouth out and then slowly sipping, letting the cool water trickle down her throat.

Eric shook his head, a wry grin on his lips. "Here," he said, handing her a couple of aspirin from the nightstand. He took the can and rinsed it out again. When he came back, he took the glass from her. "Why don't you go take a nice hot shower and I'll make you some breakfast."

"*Ummm.*" She shook her head.

"No worries." He chuckled. "How about some nice dry toast and some juice?"

Nat narrowed her eyes and Eric laughed. "Come on, Cupcake. Get in the shower. You'll feel better, I promise."

She tucked her hair behind her ear and froze, realizing she had no idea what she looked like at the moment. After the night she'd had, it couldn't be good. And the freaking hottest man in the city had been here to witness it all.

"That's probably a good idea," she murmured.

Twenty minutes later, she was showered and dressed, after a fashion. Yoga pants and her favorite sweatshirt were about as much as she could handle. She hadn't bothered with makeup. He'd seen her much worse and it didn't seem to bother him. Unless he was just hiding his disgust until he was far, far away from her. She had spent a good five minutes brushing her teeth. It had been heavenly.

And now she was sitting on the floor having her hair brushed by a surprisingly adept Eric. He got every tangle out of her hair without pulling once. She tilted her head back, enjoying the feel of his fingers running through her hair, smoothing it out after the brush ran through the strands.

"Drink some more water," he said, leaning forward to hand her the cup she'd abandoned on the coffee table.

"Bossy," she said. But she took the cup from him with a smile.

"Damn right. You need to hydrate. I think you threw up a good ninety percent of your fluids."

Nat groaned. "Don't remind me."

Eric's low chuckle stirred something in Nat that she hadn't thought was possible with how she was still feeling. Then again, since the day she'd met him, Eric had been stirring things in her she'd thought were long dead. She downed the water while Eric finished.

"There," he said, putting the brush down beside him. "You're all presentable now."

She leaned back against his legs. "Thank you."

He kissed the top of her head. "You're welcome. So, ready to hear my plans for the day?"

Nat laughed. "Sure."

"First of all," he bent down and scooped her up, "back to bed with you." He tossed her back against the pillows and handed her the remote.

"Stay here for just a minute."

"What are you up to?" Nat asked, her eyes narrowing.

"Just shush and trust me for once."

Nat smiled. "Oh-kay."

There was a knock at the door. "Stay. I'll be right back."

Eric hustled out to the front room. Nat heard him talking to someone, then heard dishes clanking in the kitchen.

"What are you doing?" she called.

"Just be patient!"

She flopped back against the pillows and looked around the room. There were signs of Eric all over. His shoes on the floor near the door. His sweatshirt on the chair in the corner. A dent in the blankets next to her where he'd been sitting. Even the slight scent of the soap he used hovered in the air of her room. And Nat liked it. Liked seeing the evidence of him in her home. It was a thought that filled her with both excitement and dread.

A few more clanks from the kitchen and a smiling Eric came in, bearing a tray laden with food. He brought it to the bed and set it up over her lap.

She looked over the selection.

"Chicken noodle soup, juice, dry whole-grain toast, applesauce, and a banana. And there's popsicles in the freezer. All foods that are good for you when you've spent the night throwing up."

"Oh they are, huh? And how do you know that?"

"I Googled it," he said, grinning.

"Oh you did, did you?"

"Of course. I'll always Google for you, Cupcake."

Nat laughed. "Wow. I'm flattered, really."

"Oh, you're laughing at me now?"

"Not at all," Nat said, not even trying to keep her amusement in check. Eric's playful side was actually rather fun when she wasn't being an anal-retentive control freak. Not that she'd ever admit that to him.

"Uh-huh. Here," he said, handing her a glass of juice. "Drink this."

Nat took it and downed half the glass. She hadn't realized how good juice could taste. "Thanks. Where's Gina?"

"She came in and checked on you last night and then left. She said to tell you she'd be at her mom's for a few days."

"*Hmm…* How did the rest of the market sale go?"

"Jared said they sold out of everything and there's great buzz about the bakery. I think we were a success. Jared said it must have been the banners he made." Eric snorted and shook his head.

"That's fantastic!" Nat said with real enthusiasm. It was wonderful that their first showing had been such a hit. Well, Eric's first showing. Still…

"Drink the rest."

She fully planned on it but his insistence had her suspicions raised. "Why?" she asked, though she went ahead and drained the glass anyway.

"Because." He took the glass and moved the tray off the bed onto the floor. "You're going to need your strength." He got back on the bed and stretched out beside her, sliding one arm over her waist.

Nat's breath caught in her throat. "I am?"

"Yes," he said, reaching for something on the other side of her. He sat back with the remote in his hand. "Because we are going to have a *Die Hard* marathon and I don't want you passing out in the middle."

Nat laughed and snuggled into him. "Bring it on."

They skipped the first one since they'd just seen it and made it through the next three *Die Hards* before breaking for more food. Nat, feeling much better, downed another bowl of soup and more toast (though Eric let her have butter on it this time). Tummy comfortably full, she leaned back with a satisfied sigh.

"Ready for *A Good Day to Die Hard*?" she asked.

Before he could answer, the front door opened and Gina called out. "Sorry! My mom had her book club over and I couldn't deal with listening to their chatter anymore."

Nat got up and poked her head out of her bedroom door. "No problem."

"You feeling better?" Gina gave her a very pointed,

amused look and Nat glared at her.

"Yeah, thanks."

Gina looked over Nat's shoulder at Eric puttering around her room and smiled. "Well, I'll just go hang out in my room or something..."

"No need," Eric said, coming up behind Nat. "How about we head to my place for a bit?"

Nat hesitated and Eric reached up to play with one of her curls. "Come on. Jared's going to some all-night World of Warcraft marathon..."

Gina snorted and rolled her eyes but Eric ignored her.

"So we'll have the whole place to ourselves. We can put *Die Hard* on the surround sound and really live it up."

Nat laughed. "Okay, let me grab my shoes."

Within thirty minutes, they were at Eric's, snuggled up in his bed. Suddenly, she could think of a lot better things to do in bed than watch a movie. Still, that was supposedly why he'd invited her over.

"Ready for the movie?" she asked, her voice low, hesitant.

Eric stretched out beside her again, bringing one hand up to brush her curls from her face.

"*Hmm*," he murmured, leaning over to trail his lips up her neck. "Maybe not just yet."

He pressed her back into the pillows and she had a sudden vision of how she must look after hanging out in her pajamas for the last day or so.

"Why don't you just let me...freshen up a bit?"

Eric shook his head and kissed her cheek. "That's girl code for 'let me go doll myself up for the next two hours.' And I can't wait that long."

He kissed the other cheek. Then lightly brushed his lips against hers.

"You can't?" she whispered.

He moaned against her neck, nuzzled against the pulse

throbbing there, his lips kissing a trail of fire up her jawline. "No," he breathed into her ear before sucking her earlobe into his mouth.

Nat gasped and arched against him, pressing her hips against the thigh he'd wedged between her legs as he lay over her.

"Besides, you're wearing sweats. I really don't think you can get any more comfortable than that."

Nat aimed a mock glare in his direction. "You know what I meant."

"Yeah, I do." Eric looked down into her eyes, smoothing her hair back from her face. He cupped her cheek, his thumb delicately tracing her eyebrow. "But you don't need to."

A small frown creased Nat's brow. Why was the nice stuff so hard to believe? Eric's thumb moved up to sweetly caress it away. "I mean it, Nat. You are so unbelievably beautiful. You take my breath away every time you walk in the room."

"Eric," Nat whispered, reaching a hand up to stroke his face.

She'd wanted to kiss him for many reasons over the past couple of months. But this was the first time the desire to touch him was a near physical pain. No man had ever said anything like that to her in her life. Yes, other men had told her she was beautiful. They'd told her they wanted her. But until now, Nat hadn't truly understood that none of them had ever really meant it. Not until she heard the words from a man who really did mean it, did she understand the difference. Eric *meant* it.

And it scared the hell out of her. But in a good way. In a way that made her want to laugh and cry and wrap her arms around him and never let him go. Nothing else going on in their lives mattered. Just him, just them, just this moment.

She leaned up, pulling on his neck to bring him down to her. She kissed him, slow and deep, her hands guiding him where she wanted him. They stripped each other, throwing their clothing away in a mindless need to feel skin on skin. Eric wrapped his arms around her waist and rolled over so she straddled him. Nat threw her head back, gasping as she rocked against him. She leaned forward, rubbing against the hard length of him from root to tip. A moan escaped her lips when he nearly slipped inside her.

"Wait…hang on…we need…in the nightstand…"

"Got it," Nat said, yanking the nightstand drawer open and handing him a condom.

Eric had it on in record time and then he reached up to pull her mouth back to his. His tongue caressed the contours of her mouth and she began to move, teasing him for a moment until she finally guided him inside her, taking him in deeper, an inch at a time.

She let out a sigh and closed her eyes as she rocked against him, her hands on his chest for support. His heart pounded against her fingers and the knowledge that it was pounding for her filled her with an indescribable emotion. Pleasure and sheer joy blended into something that bordered on ecstasy. Something that wasn't only happening because of the fire he was igniting in her body. But also because of the one he'd awakened in her heart.

The force of the sensation pulsing through her was nearly frightening in its intensity. If she thought too hard about what it meant, the fear might get the best of her. So she pushed it away. Tried to shut her brain off and just let herself *feel*. Feel Eric's hands on her body, his lips on her skin, feel the hot, solid length of him in her body.

Eric groaned and grabbed her hips, thrusting completely inside. Nat froze for a second, all thoughts banished from her mind. She luxuriated in the heat that filled her, reveled in the waves of pleasure rolling through her. Then she leaned over and trailed her lips across his skin, sucking at his earlobe, biting his neck, kissing his chest until she reached the small pebbles of his nipples. Her tongue and teeth grazed the sensitive peaks until he cried out and bucked under her.

She brought her mouth back to his, tangling one hand in his hair, forcing his tongue deeper inside her. Then she began to move, sliding up and down.

Nat threw her head back, her cries growing louder as he filled her again and again. She leaned forward so he could take her nipple in his mouth. Eric's hands moved up to her waist and she rode him, building toward a climax that hit her in pulsating waves that left her limp and drained. She collapsed on his chest, pressing a kiss to the hollow above his collarbone.

# Chapter Nineteen

Eric could feel Nat's muscles clamping around him as she came, and he exploded inside her, his hands grabbing her ass as the waves of his pleasure pumped into her. She lay on him, her sweat-soaked hair covering his chest, and he rolled to his side, taking her with him. He cradled her into his side, wrapping his arms around her. The words to tell her what she meant to him trembled on his lips. Words he'd never said to another woman in his life. Words he never thought he'd say.

But something held him back. He didn't want her to totally freak out. If she didn't feel the same way, he'd ruin what they had going for them. And he didn't want the memory of the first time they said *I love you* to each other to come on the heels of seeing her jerk-off ex. He could wait until the right moment. As long as he could go on holding her in his arms.

Drowsy as they both were, he didn't want them to wake up glued to each other or the sheets, so he rolled out of bed, ignoring Nat's protests, and went to draw them a bath.

Once he had the oversize tub filled with hot, sudsy water, he went and roused her. She glared a bit, but the promise of a hot soak, with the jets on, got her out of bed. She grabbed the sheet off the bed and wound it around herself. He cocked an eyebrow.

"Don't you think I've seen everything?"

She blushed at the reminder and he made another mental notch on the Reasons Why I Love Her list. How she could still be shy after the time they'd just had in bed together was beyond him. But it was also fucking adorable.

When she got to the tub she dropped the sheet and climbed in, sliding down with a happy sigh.

"Okay, so this wasn't such a bad idea," she said, laying her head back against the edge of the tub.

"Told you. Scootch over."

Nat sat up long enough for Eric to slip in behind her, then lay back against his chest. He wrapped his arms around her and leaned his head back, letting his eyes close.

"So, how often do you have girls staying over?" she asked.

Eric cracked open an eye, frowning down at her. "The last girl to spend the night was my ex and that was…over a year ago, I think. Why?"

Nat shrugged, a smile tugging at her lips. "You have an impressive range of bubble bath for a guy."

Eric was glad the heat of the water already had his cheeks flushed or he probably would have blushed. He did actually have an impressive collection. Though they were all what he considered manly scents. Or at least not overly feminine. It wasn't like he sat around in bubblegum or berry scented bubbles all day. *Eucalyptus and sandalwood were masculine enough scents, weren't they?* The lavender they were sitting in was just for when he'd had a particularly stressful day.

He shrugged. "It's relaxing."

"Sure. Sure. And makes you smell very pretty, too."

He splashed her a little and she giggled, nestling in closer to him. "Well, whatever your reasons, I'm glad you have it.

You're right," she said, sliding down deeper into the water. "It is very relaxing."

"Well, don't get too comfortable. Don't want you falling asleep in here."

"*Hmmm* no, that would be bad," she murmured.

They relaxed in heat-soaked silence, just enjoying the feel of the water and each other. Nat's breathing grew increasingly steady and Eric grinned. If she wasn't asleep yet, she was close. Better get her out of the tub.

"Nat. Natalie." He peeked down at her. Her eyes were closed, but he didn't think she was truly asleep just yet. "Cupcake!"

One eye cracked open. "Hush. You're disturbing me."

He chuckled and held up her hand to examine their level of prune-ishness. "I think it's about time to get out. Any longer and you might shrivel away into nothing."

She sighed. "Maybe. But it'd be a great way to go."

Eric set her away from him and stood up. Nat's mouth quirked into a small, appreciative smile as he stepped from the tub. He took his time toweling off, liking the way she watched him.

"There're fresh towels over there," he said, gesturing to them. "Take your time getting out. I'll be right back."

Nat nodded and he left her to soak. He went back into the bedroom, threw on a pair of sweatpants, and grabbed a fresh sheet from his closet. By the time Nat wandered out of the bathroom, he had the bed freshly made and had laid out a T-shirt for her to sleep in. If he'd had any doubts about his feelings for her, he would have known right then. He rarely changed the sheets for himself. But he wanted her to have a clean bed to sleep in.

She changed and slipped into bed beside him. Eric wrapped himself around her and settled down with a sigh.

"Eric," she murmured, rousing him from the brink of sleep.

"*Hmm?*"

"Thank you."

He chuckled. "I should probably be thanking you."

She laughed with him. "Not for that. Well, not just for that," she said with a shy smile. "I meant for everything. For last night. And today. For taking care of me."

"It was my very great pleasure." He pulled her back against him and kissed her on the temple. "Hey, would you like to go to a ball?"

"A what?" Nat asked, craning her neck so she could look up at him.

"A ball."

"Like a Cinderella ball?"

"Sort of," Eric said, grinning. "I have to go to this big charity fundraiser. Black tie. Dancing. Champagne."

"I don't have anything to wear."

"No worries about that." He kissed the tip of her nose. "I'll be your fairy godmother."

Nat laughed. "If you do the whole tiara and tutu thing while you're dressing me up, I'm in."

"Sorry, the tutu is at the cleaners."

"Ah, too bad," she said, little giggles still erupting from her.

"So, is it a date?" he asked, oddly nervous while he waited for her answer. He could see how the whole idea of a big, fancy ball, surrounded by his family and stuck-up friends, might be a little daunting. But he was surprised at how much he wanted her to go. How much he wanted to show her off to everyone in his life.

"Yes," she said. "I'd love to go to the ball."

"Thank you," he whispered, kissing her shoulder.

"No tiara?"

Eric laughed and pulled her closer. "No. Now go to sleep."

"Yes, Mr. Gelato."

He grinned and rested his cheek against her head. "Good night, Cupcake."

# Chapter Twenty

Nat stretched, feeling a pleasant pull in muscles that ached in a wonderful way. She rolled over. Eric still slept, his face smooth and peaceful. A soft snore escaped his lips every few seconds and Nat turned into her pillow to hide a smile he couldn't see anyway. Her bladder would force her to get up in a moment, but she wanted to stare at him for just a little longer.

He'd been so unbelievably sweet over the last couple days. She had never felt so pampered and cherished in her whole life. She didn't know where they were headed and of course they still needed to resolve things with the bakery, but for the first time, a flickering of hope that they might be able to…at the risk of sounding completely sappy…live happily ever after, filled her. Especially with a real-life fairy tale ball to get ready for.

First up, though, they needed some food. Nat eased out of bed and took care of business in the bathroom, then headed to the kitchen to see what she could whip up.

She stood in front of the open fridge, perusing the contents.

Eggs, cheese, peppers, even some ham cubes. She'd never seen a guy's fridge so well stocked. They'd have some scrumptious omelets in no time. And then, they'd unfortunately have to go to work. With the bakery opening in a few days they needed to make sure everything was ready to go.

A buzzing noise sounded from the vicinity of the toaster. It had to be Gina calling to see where she was. Nat grabbed the phone and flipped it over, her thumb swiping across the screen automatically. She realized two things mid-swipe that had her heart pounding so hard it must have bruised her chest. One, she'd just answered Eric's phone, not hers. And two, the person calling was his mother. He must have put the damn thing on vibrate so "Mamma Mia" wouldn't interrupt them.

Nat stood frozen in the middle of the kitchen, his phone in her hand, not sure what to do. She couldn't just hang up. It was his *mother*. Then again, she couldn't really talk either. That would probably not go over really well.

*Hi, yes, I'm the girl that's been in bed with your son for the last twenty-four hours. Thanks for calling.*

Yeah. Not going to happen. But she needed to do something quick. She could hear his mother (damn the woman was *loud*) calling Eric's name through the phone. She'd better run it in to him.

Mrs. Schneider's next words froze her in her tracks.

"Eric, can you hear me? Did I get your voicemail again? I didn't hear a beep. Well, look darling, I'm late for an appointment and I've only got a second. I just wanted to tell you that I'm transferring over the funds we discussed to cover the rest of your start-up costs. I ran into Courtney the other day and she's filled me in on all the details. Your father is quite adamant about buying out this food truck woman if we are going to be funding your initial costs, though. It's too much of a risk otherwise. Between what Courtney has told us and what we've found out happened with her ex-fiancé, it really would be best to wrap up whatever loose ends there are in that department as soon as possible. A hundred grand should be more than sufficient. If she refuses, offer her up to five hundred thousand. We know she can be bought, so find her price. We don't want her claiming some sort of ownership on your business. It needs to be taken care of now, before it becomes an issue. We'll send John over tomorrow morning to take care of the deed transfer and all the other paperwork. I don't want to leave matters up to that night school ninny your aunt hired. Oh, and be sure to clear your calendar for next weekend. I've invited Courtney and her parents up to the beach house for a nice little getaway."

"Nat?" Eric stood a few feet in front of her. She hadn't even heard him come in. He frowned in concern and she handed him the phone.

"It's your mother." She slapped the phone into his hand and marched back to the bedroom.

She stood trembling in the middle of Eric's room, her blood thundering in her ears. If she gave in to the anger and misery raging through her she'd smash everything in the place. She needed to remain calm. Figure out what she was going to do.

The sight of the rumpled bed they'd just left made her pause. Maybe she was overreacting. It hadn't been Eric saying those things, it had been his mother. He might be telling her off right now, defending Natalie. She should at least talk to him, find out what was going on. She pulled on her yoga pants and sweatshirt and padded quietly back to the kitchen.

She heard Eric's voice before she entered and froze.

"No, Mom, I've already asked Natalie to come with me."

Pause. Natalie could hear a raised voice from the other end of the line but couldn't make out what she was saying. Only Eric's responses.

"That's ridiculous, she'll be perfectly comfortable there."

Nat wasn't sure if she should be flattered or offended. She leaned toward offended. At least he was finally disagreeing with the woman. For her.

"I seriously doubt she's only been dating me on the off chance that I'll make her a partner," he snapped. Nat's temperature rose another few degrees.

"I don't care what you told her father, I already have a date!"

Nat's breathing grew shallow. It sounded very much like Eric's mother wanted him to escort someone else to the ball. And it really wasn't too hard to guess who.

"I don't see what Dad's merger has to do with who I date," he said. But his voice had lost some of the heat behind it. Natalie's stomach dropped.

"That's not fair. Just because you're funding my start-up expenses shouldn't mean— "

He blew out a frustrated breath of air and jammed his fingers through his hair. "I can't believe you're making me do this."

Natalie closed her eyes against the tears that threatened. It couldn't be happening again. Not after everything they'd just shared.

Eric sighed, a defeated sound that ricocheted through Natalie like a piece of heated steel. "Fine. Tell Courtney I'll pick her up at eight."

Eric dropped his phone to the counter and Natalie sucked in a tremulous breath. The sound of his fist making contact with some hard surface made her jump.

All the tender moments of the last day flew through her mind, each one now cast in the ugly light of betrayal. It had felt so real. So natural. So wonderful. And it had all been a lie. The second Mommy put her foot down Eric had obeyed, despite what doing so would do to Natalie. The back-up plan was no longer needed. His parents would never approve of him keeping his little stray, especially when a thoroughbred was ready and waiting. And after all, Nat could be bought off. Right? And Eric had just proven yet again that he'd do what his parents wanted. She should have known better. She *had* known better. She'd just let herself get sucked into the fantasy.

A lump formed in her throat and her eyes burned with tears she refused to let fall. No. She wasn't going to make some big scene this time. She wasn't going to scream and cry and make a total fool of herself. Not like she'd done when Steve had walked out on her. This time she'd keep some dignity. The lump in her throat grew and she swallowed, trying to ease the pressure. She'd thought she'd known what it felt like to have her heart break. And she did. This…this was so much worse. Her heart wasn't breaking; it was shattering into a million pieces.

She had to get out of there. She would *not* let him see her cry…again.

Nat walked through the kitchen, ignoring Eric when he called her name. She ran down the stairs and grabbed her boots from near the door, shoving her feet into them a little more forcefully than necessary. Eric followed her, calling her name, but he couldn't follow her outside in nothing but his boxer briefs. She opened the door and forced herself to take deep breaths. She could lose it when she got home. Not until then.

"Natalie!"

Nat's eyes flew open and through her tear-blurred vision she caught a brief glimpse of Eric at the top of the stairs. She closed the door and bolted. Eric looked beaten, stricken even. Her head spun with confusion. It took a special kind of asshole to pull off what Eric had apparently been pulling. But up until fifteen minutes earlier, Nat would have bet everything that whatever had been between them had been real. And that was the real bitch of it, wasn't it? She had bet everything. Her business. Her heart. Her soul. And she'd lost. There was no way she was going to sit around and let him, or his parents, gloat over it. Not while it was still a raw wound that seared her with pain every time she took a breath.

She took off down the street at a brisk walk. She had a few minutes on him. He'd had nothing but a blanket wrapped around his waist. He'd have to get dressed before coming after her. If he even bothered to come. Just in case, she took the scenic route home, cutting through an alley or two until she was sure he couldn't follow her trail. Nat let her breath out, impatiently dashing away the tears that came with it.

Her phone rang. Eric. It kept blaring from the recesses of her purse. Nat hit Ignore. She couldn't talk to him yet. She would. But not yet. The phone rang again. Ignore. Again. Ignore. By the time she reached her apartment, she gave up and just shut the damn thing off.

She hauled her sorry butt up the stairs to her apartment. Gina met her at the door, phone in her hand, mouth open ready to interrogate her. But one look at Natalie's face and Gina zipped it, pulling her inside.

"Who do I need to kill?"

Nat snorted through her tears. She could always count on Gina. "No one. I'm fine."

"This," Gina said, waving at Nat, "isn't fine. What the hell did Eric do?"

"It's my own damn fault."

"Doubtful."

Gina's phone rang and she glanced at the screen. "It's Eric. He's called twice already asking if you've showed up here."

"Ignore him."

Gina hit Ignore and tossed her phone onto the counter. "Spill it. He's worried sick."

Nat shook her head. "Yeah. I'm sure he is."

Gina folded her arms. Nat took a deep breath and filled her in.

"That...that...fucking asshole!" she said, once Nat had finished.

"Yeah."

"Had he mentioned anything about buying you out, at all?"

Nat paused, the money his mother had mentioned having momentarily slipped her mind in the aftermath of Eric shoving her aside for his parents' pick of the litter.

"No. Never."

Gina shook her head. "It doesn't make any sense."

"What doesn't? We knew from day one he wanted that garage."

"Yeah, but..."

"But what?"

"I don't know. It just seemed like you two were getting along so well."

"Yeah. I thought so, too. But, he must have just been using me until he could talk his parents into giving him the money or something. He was certainly using me for something else. His parents are never going to approve of me and that seems to be all that matters to him."

"Ah sweetie." Gina pulled her in for a hug.

They sat on the couch and Nat finally let go. She let the tears come, let the pain pour out. And God it hurt like nothing she'd ever felt before. This is why she'd closed herself off for so long. She'd never wanted to feel this kind of pain again, and yet there she was, feeling her heart disintegrate, one little piece at a time.

When she'd finally cried herself out, Gina stood and went to get her a bottle of water. Nat went into the bathroom and splashed cold water on her face. Her eyes were already red and swollen, but the water helped a bit. Until she caught the faint scent of Eric and realized she still wore his T-shirt. Tears threatened to erupt again, but she choked them back this time. She was done crying over him. Nat came back out of the bathroom and gratefully downed the water Gina held out to her.

A knock at the door had them both glaring before they even heard Eric call out.

"Nat? You there?"

Gina looked at her. "What do you want me to do? Want me to get rid of him?"

Nat took a deep breath and wiped her eyes. "No. Might as well get this over with."

Gina frowned but went to open the door. Eric barreled right past her on a beeline for Nat. He reached out to touch her but she backed up and he dropped his hand, a frown creasing his forehead.

"Nat, look, I know we need to talk. You obviously overheard... I wanted to explain but you didn't answer my calls."

"You've got a lot of nerve showing up here, you son of a bitch," Gina said.

Eric turned to her, glaring. "No offense, Gina, but butt the hell out. I came here to talk to Natalie, not you."

Before Gina could retaliate, Nat held up her hand. "It's okay, Gina. I'll take care of it."

Gina sent Eric another death look but headed to her bedroom. "I'll be in here if you need me."

Nat nodded and turned to Eric, her arms crossed across her stomach as though physically holding herself together might help her keep a grip on her emotions.

"Why did you leave? Why did you just walk out without a word? I know you must have heard about the ball. But we could have talked..." Eric asked.

"What good does talking do? The only people you listen

to are your parents. And you screwing me over for another woman isn't the only issue here. Are you really not even going to mention the money your mom just gave you to buy me out? Or the whole *we won't fund your costs unless you get rid of her because she's too big a risk* thing?"

Eric's frown deepened. "None of that was my idea. I didn't agree to any of it."

"Oh, don't give me that," Nat snapped, her tenuous hold on her emotions fraying further at his dodge. "You've wanted that garage since the second you realized your aunt left it to me. I just didn't realize you'd stoop so low to get it."

"What the hell are you talking about?"

"You know you wanted it!"

"Yes, I did, but you obviously think I've done something about it and it would be really nice if you'd share just what exactly I'm supposed to have done because I have no fucking clue why you are so pissed at me!"

"I'm pissed because I don't like being used! If you wanted to buy me out, all you had to do is say so."

"You said you wouldn't sell."

Nat's heart dropped. "So you did want to buy me out."

"I already told you, I don't have the money to do that. My parents never said a word about funding me until that phone call. And we came to our little compromise, which I thought was working great, so I never brought it up with them again. If you had an issue with our arrangement, why didn't you say something?"

"I didn't think I needed to. You knew how I felt about selling."

"Right. Which is why nothing you are saying is making any sense."

"So you expect me to believe that your mother just decided, out of the blue, to give you the money you need to 'buy out that food truck woman'? You know, if you wanted me gone, all you had to do was say so. I never wanted your bakery. All I wanted was to be able to keep my garage and maybe rent some kitchen space from you. I wasn't ever trying to cheat or con you out of anything. We could have kept to ourselves; we didn't need to have any more contact than necessary. But no, you decided you'd just sit back and let me do all the work getting the bakery up and running and right when it's ready to launch, you just swoop in with a big old check to buy me out of my garage and make me go away. And hell, why not have a little fun on the side, too? Might as well get a piece of ass while you're at it, right?"

Eric stepped closer. "My God, Natalie, you can't possibly believe that! That is *not* what happened. I don't know what Courtney is doing talking to my mother, or what she told her about you or the bakery."

"While we're at it, why don't you tell me the truth for once about Courtney? Is she your girlfriend? Fiancée?"

"I already told you she's not!"

"Well, I'm sorry if I don't believe you, but there's obviously more to your relationship than just an old family friend if a few words from her to your mother lands a hundred grand in your lap! Not to mention the fact that you can't seem to stop dumping me the second she wants you for something."

"Nat, I didn't lie to you about Courtney or anything else. I only agreed to take her to the ball because my dad needs to impress his investors, the chief of whom is Courtney's father. I don't have a choice. As for the rest, I don't know what the hell is going on. Yes, I'd asked my parents for the money to get things running but they hadn't said anything for the past two months—until this morning. There were certainly no conditions of you leaving when we first discussed it. And I never thought or said that you would try to come back and try to claim ownership."

"How am I supposed to believe that?"

"Because you know me, Nat."

Nat stared at him, wanting to believe him. But the timing was incredibly suspicious. Now that all the work was done and the bakery was ready to open, suddenly his mother hands him the money he needs to get rid of her? And being thrown over for Courtney or any woman wasn't something she was prepared to forgive. A knock sounded at the door and Nat blew out a breath. Who the hell could that be?

She stomped over and yanked the door open. A surprised-looking courier stood there with a thick envelope in his hands.

"Miss Natalie Moran?" he asked.

"Yes."

"These are for you." He handed her the envelope and took off before Nat could ask what it was.

She stuck her finger under the glued flap and ripped it open, pulling out a thick sheaf of folded papers from a law firm. She read through them quickly, her eyesight beginning to blur again as the words "injunction," "cease all use," "pending appeal" and other phrases signaled the end of all her hard work and dreams.

Nat looked up at Eric, her face a frozen mask. Eric took a step closer.

"Nat…"

"Get out," she said, her words barely more than a whisper.

"What?"

She held up the papers. "An injunction from your family's lawyer, on behalf of his client, Mr. Eric Gerard Schneider, that prohibits me from using the garage until such time as the appeal of your aunt's will has been heard in court."

"What?" Eric's face paled and he took a step toward her. "Nat…I didn't…"

"Get. Out."

"I didn't do this, Nat. I mean, I agreed to them looking into the will, but that was before. I didn't think…"

Nat threw the papers at him. "It's your name on those papers, Eric! What, it wasn't enough to just lie to me and use me, you had to go and take everything from me? I guess your precious lawyer found a way around buying me out, didn't he?"

"Nat…"

"I can't believe you'd do this! I thought you were different. You acted all noble. The hardworking black sheep, going against his family to make his own way in the world, right? But instead you are just a spoiled little trust fund brat. You didn't get your way so you ran to your rich mommy to bail you out. I should have known that whole 'I want to do it on my own' routine was a load of shit when I saw your house."

"That is not what happened!"

"Oh, that's right, the house was from your grandparents. That makes it much better."

"You are such a hypocrite! I'm a spoiled little rich boy for taking the brownstone my grandparents left me when they died, but it's perfectly acceptable for you to take the garage my aunt left you?"

"That's different and you know it."

"No, it's not! And it's not even the point. Where I live has nothing to do with anything."

"No, you're right. The point is you lied and manipulated me to get what you wanted and when that didn't work you asked your parents to throw some money at it. Well, you can't buy me, Eric!"

"I'm not trying to buy you, I didn't even know about that money."

"You used me—"

"I didn't use you any more than you used me! You seem to forget that you were getting something out of this deal too. You agreed to help for free kitchen time—"

"Free? I worked my ass off for the right to use your

kitchen. You wouldn't even have a kitchen to use if it wasn't for me. And the second the bakery is up and running and you don't need me anymore, the money you need to get rid of me just magically falls in your lap. Kind of a strange coincidence, don't you think? I'm not some gold digger just looking for a payday. Do you have any idea how insulting this all is?"

"Would you just listen?"

"Listen to what? You can't excuse this, Eric."

"I know there's no excuse for it, but it was just a mistake. I didn't think any of this would happen. My dad suggested looking into you and challenging the will and I said yes just to get him off my back. I didn't think they'd be able to do anything about it and I certainly didn't think they'd find anything on you that would concern them. And while I may not agree with their conclusions, I'm sorry but I can see why they might be concerned. The situations are a little too similar."

An icy chill ran through Nat's blood and settled like a hard ball in the pit of her stomach. "What situations?"

Eric's eyes searched hers for a moment and then he blew out a frustrated breath. "When you try to claim something that isn't yours until you get a check big enough to make you go away."

Nat's breath left her in a rush, like he had hauled back and sucker punched her in the gut. "You know about that? What did you guys do, have me investigated? What gives you the right to go digging into my life?"

"It wasn't my choice, but honestly I didn't think it would matter because I assumed there'd be nothing to find. Instead, they find out you seem to have a sort of habit of…"

"Of what? Working my ass off with someone I thought was my partner and then getting screwed? Because from my view point that's the only thing happening here. How dare you—"

"For the hundredth time, I didn't run the background

checks. My parents did. They were just looking out for me and apparently they had a reason to be concerned. You have to admit, it looks bad, Nat. What am I supposed to think?"

"You are supposed to trust me! These situations are nothing alike. I wrote that cookbook that Steve published. Every page. Every recipe is mine. He stole it. He put his name on it. And because he was the first one to turn it in, I got screwed! Trying to prove intellectual property is next to impossible, especially when he had a whole team of high-priced lawyers on his side. So yes, I took money from him, even though it was far less than what he actually owed me and I only took it because he'd taken everything else from me and I needed to survive. I wanted to start over. So when he offered me half of the advance money for *my* book, I took it. But I certainly didn't try and con some poor victim out of something I had no right to. And I definitely wouldn't have done it to you!"

Eric shoved a hand through his hair. "Nat, I didn't—"

"No. You know what, Eric, I'm done. This," she said, waving her hands between them, "whatever *this* is, it's over. Done. Just go."

"Natalie, you can't just throw me out. This was just a stupid mistake that never should have happened. Just wait—"

"No! I'm done. Get out!" Nat screamed.

Gina came running, took one look at Nat's face and advanced on Eric with murder in her eyes. Eric held up his hands and backed toward the door.

"Fine, I'll leave, but this isn't over, Nat. I'm going to fix this."

Gina slammed the door in his face and Nat collapsed on the couch.

"Oh, God," Nat murmured, her head dropping into her hands.

She wanted to be strong, wanted to be the ballsy heroine

she always saw in the movies. The type that gets into an impossible scrape but is able to pull herself up and outwit the bad guys. But that was fiction and this was real life. And Nat just didn't see any way of winning this one.

She had no lawyer, no money to pay for one, no way to fight what had just happened. And she didn't have the right kind of background or bank account to fight for Eric. No way to make his parents approve of her. No desire to make them approve of her, if she were honest. If he didn't love her enough to fight for her, stand up to his parents, they had no chance, anyway.

What hurt worse than anything was that even though her dreams of a better business, a better life, were crumbling around her, the thing that made her ache as though she'd been beaten, was the loss of Eric. He was what filled her thoughts. His betrayal was making her want to howl and scream and cry.

Gina sat beside her and pulled her into a hug. Nat sank into her. She wanted to be strong, but right at that moment, it was just too much to bear. She'd be strong later. But first, she was going to fall completely apart.

# Chapter Twenty-One

Eric pulled out his phone as he stomped down the stairs from Nat's apartment. He dialed his mother's number three times. No answer. He didn't bother trying his father. It was doubtful he'd answer at this time of day. He was surely in some meeting or other.

He drove to the bakery. Jared waited impatiently inside.

"Hey, where have you been? You were supposed to be here an hour ago."

"Yeah, well, nothing's going like it's supposed to today." He marched out to the garage, Jared trailing behind him. A large chain was padlocked around the door handles. And Nat's truck was inside.

"Do you know anything about this?" Eric asked.

Jared shook his head. "Not a clue. Who would lock it up?"

"Damn blood-sucking lawyers."

"What are you talking about?"

Eric went to the supply closet in the back of the bakery, filling Jared in while he rummaged through the old tools piled in the corner.

"So, your mom is giving you the money to buy the garage?"

Eric glared but didn't answer.

"That's good, right? I mean, that's what you wanted isn't it?"

Eric stopped. Was it what he wanted? Maybe at first. Yes, he'd wanted the garage, wanted full control of the entire building. But now? Images of a halo of hazelnut curls and flashing golden eyes danced through his mind. Screw the garage. Screw the bakery. He just wanted Nat.

"Dammit." He'd hoped there'd be a pair of bolt cutters or something stashed away so he could get rid of the lock before Nat saw it. "I gotta go," he said, heading back to where his car was parked.

"Wait! What do you mean, you've got to go? This place opens in days. Your brand new employees will be here for orientation and training in thirty minutes. You can't leave!"

"Here." Eric tossed him the manager's hat. "You just got promoted."

Jared stared dumbfounded at Eric. "Are you insane? I'm just the guy who designed your logo and painted your signs."

"You'll do great. I have total faith in you."

"Well, good for you. But I don't!"

"Sorry, man. I've got some stuff to take care of. I've got to go find some cutters to get that damn lock off the garage. If Natalie comes before I get back, you have my permission to break the doors down if you need to, whatever you have to do to get her truck out. Hopefully, I'll make it back before she sees that," he said, jerking his head at the padlocked doors. He jumped back in his car. "Then I've got to take a little trip out to the beach house and have a talk with my mother, since she's refusing to answer her phone. I've got to get this mess cleared up."

Jared stared at him a moment. Then a slow smile spread

across his face. "Ah dude. You love her, don't you?"

Eric stared back, then snorted and shook his head like he was trying to clear it. "Yeah. I do."

Jared put the apron on and stepped away from the car. "Go get her, man. I'll take care of things here."

"Thanks, Jared. Really."

Jared nodded. "Oh, and don't worry about the padlock. I can pick that thing, piece of cake."

Eric opened his mouth to ask how the hell Jared knew how to pick a padlock and then changed his mind. He really didn't want to know. "Great. Just get it off the door."

"On it!" Jared gave Eric a goofy salute and jogged back toward the garage.

Eric shook his head again and pulled away from the curb.

For the entire long drive to his parents' beach house, scenes with Nat ran through his head. The way she'd looked when she had tripped and shoved his gelato up his nose the day they'd met, or later, covered in chocolate sprinkles with a swollen cheek. Her flashing eyes when they'd argued. Her laugh, the little snort at the end when she really got going, so full of life and happiness that he couldn't help but join in. Even pale and sick, her beauty had taken his breath away. He loved her. Every inch of her. Every little quirk. Even her obsessive need to alphabetize everything within reach. Or her refusal to buy an odd number of anything. Or her disturbing habit of tripping over her own feet. He loved her. And he was going to fix this. No matter what it cost him.

He'd already lost the most important thing in the world to him. Nothing else mattered.

By the time he pulled into his parents' house, the sun was beginning to set. Jared had texted that all had gone well with the employees, and that he'd gotten the lock off the garage. But Nat hadn't shown up.

He parked his car, ignoring the throngs of his parents'

friends filtering into the house and the strange looks he got at his extremely informal attire. Another one of his mother's interminable dinner parties, no doubt. Well, they'd just have to put the party on hold for a few minutes.

He marched inside, going from room to room, looking for his mother. Unfortunately, the first person he ran into was Courtney.

"Eric, darling," she said, reaching for him.

He stepped out of her reach and looked past her. "Have you seen my mother?"

"Well, hello to you, too," she said, her face set in a pissy pout.

"What did you tell my mother about Natalie?"

"Who?"

"You know very well who she is. My mother said you filled her in on all the details. What exactly did you tell her?"

"I just told her what was going on. How that little tramp was trying to take advantage of you like she'd done with your aunt."

Eric fumed, but tried to keep a rein on his anger. Shouting at Courtney in the middle of a party was not the way to get on his mother's good side.

"What is going on between me and Nat is no one's business but ours. Not my mother's and certainly not yours."

Courtney's mouth curled up in disgust. "She's obviously got you thinking with something other than the head on your shoulders or you would have taken care of this little situation a long time ago. I was just trying to help you out."

"No, you weren't." Eric seethed and took a deep breath to calm down. Courtney was nothing more than a vindictive little harpy, but he wasn't going to stoop to her level to inform her of that. "You were pissed that I didn't want you and did your best to ruin who I *did* want."

Courtney sputtered, her face flushing in anger. But

before she could make an even bigger scene than they were already making, Eric turned his back on her and went to find his mother. He was done wasting time on Courtney and her nonsense.

His mother's laugh from the deck drew him outside. She stood surrounded by her friends, holding court like a queen. She caught sight of him and her eyes widened in surprise. She handed her champagne to a passing waiter and came toward him.

"Hello, dear," she said, grasping his shoulders in a quick hug. She stepped back, her gaze raking him from head to toe, taking in his rumpled sweatpants and T-shirt and tousled hair. Eric hadn't realized until just then how bad he must look. He should have taken the time to at least throw on some jeans or something, but when he'd woken and watched Nat run from him, he hadn't given a thought to anything else. And the rest of the revelations of the day had dropped a change of clothes to the bottom of his list of priorities.

"That's an interesting outfit," she said, her lips grazing his cheek. "You look like you just rolled out of bed." Before he could speak, she brushed past him. "My office."

They entered her office from the French doors on the patio, not speaking until she had the doors closed firmly behind them. "Now. To what do I owe the pleasure of you crashing my soiree?"

"Natalie Moran."

His mother's eyebrow raised slightly. "What about her? I thought we took care of that. Does she want more money?"

Eric raked his hand through his hair. "No, Mother. She doesn't want money. Neither do I. Why would you send me money to buy her out? I never asked you to do that."

"Of course not. You're as stubborn as your father. So when Courtney told me about your little situation and how clingy the girl was getting, I decided to save you the trouble of asking and just help you out. It's much more than the garage is worth. It's a good deal for her."

Eric took a breath. He knew his mother's intentions had been in the right place. And he'd been raised to be respectful. But damn if he didn't want to rip his hair out by the roots.

"I appreciate the thought, but I really don't need you to bail me out. Natalie and I have an agreement that is working out fine. I have no desire to take the garage from her."

The other eyebrow went up. "Why on earth not? The whole situation is ridiculous. I don't know what your aunt was thinking."

Eric had an inkling, and highly suspected it had more to do with matchmaking than with baking, but he wasn't going to get into that with his mother. "It doesn't matter, Mom. What matters is that the bakery is my business and I am running it the way I decided was best. Like I said, I appreciate you sending the money, but I don't need it. I'm not going to buy Nat out. And I want you to call your lawyers and get the appeal dropped. Tonight."

Eric's mother leaned against her desk, her gaze boring into him. He resisted the urge to squirm. When she stared at him like that it had always seemed like his mother could look into his very soul and read the thoughts in his head.

"You love her," she said.

Eric started, for a split second thinking that maybe she *had* read his mind. And for another second, he considered denying it. But the slight smile on his mother's lips let him know there'd be no point in that.

"Yes."

"Nonsense," his father said, coming in from the hallway.

"Dad."

His dad held up his hand. "Enough. The situation has already been taken care of, there's no reason to rehash it."

"What do you mean, no reason? You can't just…"

Eric stopped, suddenly acutely aware that he was about to defy his parents for the first time in his life. Oh he'd pushed them on small stuff, sure. He'd made choices they wouldn't approve of, frequently. But he'd never outright defied them. Never said *no*. Never gone against their opinion, on anything. He wasn't going to lie that the thought of doing it now was making him a bit queasy. But he'd go through a lot worse for Natalie.

"I can and I have. The discussion is over. Now, John will be in touch once the buyout is complete and—"

"No."

Eric's father stopped, one eyebrow raised in cool surprise. "Excuse me?"

"I said no," Eric repeated, standing as straight and tall as he could. It was probably the most difficult thing he'd ever done, but he looked his father right in the eye and said it again. "No. There will be no buyout. No sale. No break up. I'm keeping the bakery. I'll be quitting my job and running it full time. With Natalie at my side. In whatever capacity she likes. As my wife, if she'll have me. As my business partner, no matter what."

"Eric," his mother said, her eyes wide with shock and surprise.

"Are you finished?" his father asked.

"Yes, sir." Eric met his father's gaze. And waited.

"Good. Now, let me tell you what's really going to happen. You will let John go ahead with the sale of the bakery and you will go back to your job so that you can utilize the education that I paid for. Next summer, you will join me at my firm, as planned. As for this…girl…you will end it. Immediately. You know what we've found out about her. I will not invest so much money in something that is already a huge risk when someone with her reputation is involved. I would prefer you come to your senses and get out of this whole bakery business entirely. But at the very least, you need to cut off your association with this woman. I have invested too much in your future to let you throw it away."

"I'm not some investment, Dad. I'm your son."

"Yes. You are. So start acting like it. What's it going to be?"

Eric paused, drawing deep breaths in through his tight throat, anger and pain flooding through him. He didn't believe it had come to this. This wasn't what he wanted. But he couldn't go through with what his father asked.

"I love you and Mom. I appreciate everything you've ever done for me, more than I'll ever be able to say. But this is *my* life. I hoped you would understand. Support me. But if you are asking me to choose between your money and the woman I love…"

"I shouldn't think it would be much of a choice."

Eric looked down, braced himself for what he was about to say. "You're right. It's not."

He went to his mother, kissed her cheek. "I love you, Mom."

Then he went to the door. "I love you, too, Dad. And I'm sorry I'm ruining all the plans you'd made. I truly am. But I need to do what I feel is best for me. I'll get my business going. On my own. I believe what Natalie's told me about what happened in her past. I trust her. She's my life."

He left then, unbearable sadness filling him at the hurt in his father's eyes. He'd just crushed the dream his father had had for him since the day he was born. The company he'd spent his whole life building so he could share it with his son would fall to other hands someday. Causing the man who'd given him so much any sort of disappointment was the hardest thing he'd ever done. Hopefully, someday his father would understand. Because giving up Natalie would have destroyed Eric. He was going to get her back, no matter what he had to do. Because living without her was not an option.

# Chapter Twenty-Two

Eric was woken up at the crack of dawn by the *Iron Man* theme song blaring from his phone. *Jared.* Eric grabbed the phone and growled into it. "Seriously? The sun isn't even up yet. What are you even doing awake? And more importantly, why the hell are you calling and waking me up?"

"I came down to the bakery to paint the rest of your signage."

Eric grunted. Jared actually on time for a job? Amazing. "What do you need?"

There was a slight pause. "I think you should come down here."

"I'm still down the shore."

"What are you doing down there?"

"Things didn't go well with my parents last night. So I got drunk and then I got a hotel. What do you need? It's only four thirty in the morning. I'll be back later this morning. Can it wait?"

Another pause.

"Jared, what's going on?"

"Natalie's been down here, I think."

Eric sat up, fully awake. "What do you mean?"

"Her truck is gone. I got the chain off the doors like you said, but the truck was still there when I left last night. It's not here now."

"Well, that's not unusual. She or Gina probably just took it out for the daily run."

"It's too early for that."

"Is her other stuff gone? Do you think it was stolen?"

"No. But…everything of hers that was down here is gone. Her apron, that big whisk she liked. Even those stupid oven mitts. And…she left something here for you. An envelope. It was taped to the garage doors."

Eric was already up and throwing on his shoes. "I'm leaving now. I'll be there as soon as I can."

He hung up the phone and grabbed his car keys. Then he hopped in his car and hauled ass.

What could she have left him? If she'd wanted to talk to him, she could have called or texted or, hell, even emailed him. He seriously doubted it was some old-fashioned love letter. Whatever it was, he probably wasn't going to like it. And he had a really bad feeling he already knew what it was.

Two hours later, Eric stood staring at the glaringly empty garage. Jared had left the envelope where Nat had taped it to the inside of one of the doors. A large manila envelope with his name scrawled on it in Nat's distinctive handwriting. He didn't want to touch it. It felt disturbingly like he had come home to find an empty apartment and divorce papers waiting for him.

Once he finally ripped the thing down and opened it, he found he hadn't been entirely wrong. Nat had signed ownership of the garage over to him. All the legal documents were here, neatly signed, with a formal letter relinquishing all rights to the property and waiving any future claims to the bakery or garage. There was also a receipt and work order papers from the auto shop that had fixed his car, with a warranty in case they'd missed something. And a brand new shirt, presumably to replace the one she'd ruined the day they'd met, was hanging from a hook on the wall. All links to him carefully tied up. And severed.

But there was no note from her. Nothing that explained why she was giving up the garage. Nothing about where she was or what she was going to do. Or if she'd ever be back. Though the removal of all her personal items seemed to answer that question.

Eric's heart sank and he cleared his throat, trying to ease the sudden tightness.

Jared's hand clapped on his shoulder. "I'm sorry, man. But…at least you got what you wanted. Right?"

Eric frowned. "Did I?"

"Sure. I mean, you wanted the garage, right?"

"Yeah."

"Well." Jared shrugged.

Eric's shoulders slumped and he turned to go back into the bakery. He looked around. It was amazing. Gleaming cases ready for trays of sweetness. Tables and chairs waiting for customers. Polished ovens and equipment restored to their former beauty with enough modern touches to make everything as efficient as possible. Everything was pristine and perfect. And it was all her. None of it would have been possible without her.

He didn't want it without her. It meant nothing without her.

Eric slapped the papers on the counter and looked at Jared, who was grinning at him like a drunk monkey.

"Go get your girl," Jared said.

Eric laughed. "I wish it was going to be that easy. I think I've got a plan, though."

"Lay it on me, man. I'm all in."

"Good. Because I'm going to need all the help I can get."

. . .

Gina stood at the door, blocking Eric from coming into the apartment.

"I just want to talk to her, Gina. It's been almost a month and she still won't return my calls. She hasn't been down to the bakery at all, not even on opening day. She hasn't been working with you in the truck. I'm worried about her."

"She's fine."

"When will she be back? I'll wait."

"I don't know what her plans are. She went out to visit her parents in Pennsylvania. She's been talking about opening a bakery near her mom's place."

"She *what*?" Eric nearly shouted.

Gina sighed. "She's destroyed, Eric. You really did a number on her, pulling that shit."

"That's why I need to talk to her. I didn't *do* anything. It was my parents and I've taken care of it. They won't interfere again. She should have heard from their lawyer by now, so she knows the will is not being contested. And I ripped up the papers she left. The garage is still hers to use. I haven't touched it and have no plans to do so."

"I'll tell her," Gina said, trying to shut the door again.

"Wait," Eric said, shoving his foot in the door.

"Get your foot out of the door, Eric. I have a marble rolling pin in the kitchen and I have zero problem using it on whatever part of your anatomy I think will cause you the most pain."

"Just…just tell her to call me. Please. We need to talk. I want to tell her…" Eric sighed and shoved his fingers through his hair. "Tell her the bakery is open and doing fantastic and it's all due to her. Ask her to come down to see it. Please. There's something she needs to see. Things to discuss. And, tell her I miss her. Tell her…" He sighed again.

"I'll tell her," Gina said again, her voice now softer, almost sympathetic.

Eric nodded, his head hanging in defeat. This time he let Gina close the door.

Gina came back into the bedroom and sat on the bed beside Natalie. "Did you hear all that?"

"Yeah," Nat said, defeat filling her own voice.

She'd been trying so hard to hate him. Been trying to forget all the sweet moments, all the laughter, the sense of absolute rightness when he touched her. But frankly, Eric was impossible to forget. She'd managed to avoid him over the last few weeks, but just hearing his voice at the door made her tremble. She wanted him, more than anything or anyone else she had ever wanted in her life.

She liked how she was when she was with him. He somehow brought out the best in her, even when they were arguing. From the moment she'd danced for him at the club, to the last night they'd spent together, Eric had inspired something in her, something she hadn't felt for a long time. He'd helped her find her confidence in herself again. Every time he'd looked at her with desire and admiration shining from his eyes, a little of what Steve had destroyed had been rebuilt. She liked who she was when she was with him, and who he was when he was with her. They were better together.

Nat had pushed Eric away, tried to shut off that part of her that wanted to believe someone like him could really want someone like her. But why the hell shouldn't he want her? She was smart, funny, had ample proof that she was sexy as hell, at least in his eyes and that was all she cared about, and she could bake a damn good cupcake, too. She wanted him, plain and simple. And maybe that wasn't such a bad thing.

Maybe she could have her cake and eat it, too. Why the hell shouldn't she be happy? Maybe she really could have it all.

"For what it's worth," Gina said, "I think he means it. I don't think he had anything to do with that whole mess with the lawyers and money. I don't think he was just using you."

Nat's head jerked up. Gina was the last person to defend Eric.

"Really?"

"Really." Gina reached out and took her hand. "Did you ever open that letter from the lawyers that was waiting when you got back from your mom's?"

Nat frowned. "No. I figured it was more paperwork about the will and I just didn't have the energy to deal with it."

"I think you should see what it says. Eric said the will was no longer being contested."

"What?"

Nat jumped up and pulled the letter out of the drawer where she'd shoved it. She opened and skimmed it quickly, a sense of relief filling her. Along with a sinking depression. He'd called it off. Immediately. The letter was dated the day she'd left for her mom's, the day after he'd come to see her and they'd had that horrible fight. He'd been telling the truth. He hadn't had anything to do with it and he'd done what he could to fix everything…the second he had found out.

She suddenly felt like the biggest bitch in the world. *What have I done?*

Gina continued. "And I don't see any money lying around here, so he obviously didn't force you to sell. I think he's telling the truth about the garage, about not using it. They've been turning down any delivery orders because they don't have a truck yet."

"How do you know that?"

Gina grimaced. "Jared. He called the other day. I didn't hang up. Don't you dare say a word!" she said, holding up a hand to wave off the thousands of questions that suddenly crowded Nat's brain. *Jared and Gina? Wow.*

"There's something else you should probably know. I wasn't sure whether I should tell you or not, but…well…"

"What?"

"Eric's parents cut him off."

"What?"

"Jared said they told him to sell the bakery and give you up or he'd be cut off. Not really disowned, I don't think. But they certainly aren't funding anything. He refused to play by their rules. He chose you over his family."

Nat pulled her legs up to her chest and wrapped her arms around them, leaning her head on her knees.

"I can't believe he did that. What would I even say to him? After all the horrible things I said."

"He hasn't stopped calling, has he? And he even came over here and braved my wrath," Gina said with a smile. "He wants to talk to you, Nat."

Nat closed her eyes. "I'm afraid," she said, her voice barely audible. A few tears fell from her lashes and Gina held up the corner of the sheet so Nat could wipe them away.

"I know you are, babe. But he isn't Steve. Not even close. I think he might actually be a decent guy. But don't you dare tell him I said that."

Nat smiled, the dark weight that had been crushing her for weeks finally lifting enough so she could breathe.

Okay. She wasn't going to hold her breath over it, but she'd at least go see him, hear him out. He had called off the lawyers. Whether it was because he'd had a change of heart or it hadn't been his doing in the first place, the important point was that he'd called them off. Right? And in all fairness she'd set out to use him, too. It was supremely unfair for her to judge him for something she'd also done. She'd just been too hurt to acknowledge that, until now. Until she'd heard his voice, the emotion behind it, when he hadn't known she could hear him.

Okay. She'd go. And pray to God she didn't end up hurting worse than she already did.

# Chapter Twenty-Three

Eric packed a box with a dozen cannoli and an order of chocolate-drizzled baklava and handed it to the customer who waited.

"Thank you, come again," he said.

He grabbed an empty tray and carried it into the back. Jared stood at the back door, hanging half outside.

"Jared, what are you doing?" he called over his shoulder while he put the tray in the sink. "We're getting slammed out there."

Jared popped his head back in. "Someone's here to see you, boss."

Eric turned around at the odd note in his friend's voice. Nat walked through the door and Eric sucked in a breath.

"Nat."

She gave him a hesitant smile. "Hey."

Jared looked back and forth between them. "I'll, uh, just go take care of things out front."

He gave them a huge grin and hurried back to the front counter.

Eric walked toward Nat slowly, afraid if he moved too fast she'd take off.

"I wanted to explain…"

She held up a hand and shook her head. "You don't need to. I realize you didn't ask your parents for that money. And I got the papers about the appeal. Thank you. I'm sorry it took so long. I was out of town for a while."

He took another few steps closer. "I got your papers, too."

Nat ducked her head and Eric closed the distance between them, standing close enough to touch her, though he didn't. Not yet. "I shredded them."

She looked up at him. "Why?"

"I don't want the garage." He finally reached out and smoothed a thumb over her cheek. "I want you."

Nat released a tremulous breath and stepped into his arms. "I want you, too," she said, wrapping her arms around him.

He pressed her head to his shoulder, kissed her forehead. "God, I missed you."

"I missed you, too."

She rose up on tiptoes so she could kiss him.

Their lips met and Eric groaned, crushing her to him, trying to mold her body to his. He poured every ounce of love and desperation he'd felt over the last few weeks into that kiss. Let her feel how much he needed her. She returned it with everything she had, her lips moving over his, her arms clutching him to her like she was afraid he'd disappear if she let go. He knew how she felt.

When they finally came up for air, Eric wrapped his arms around her and just held her, enjoying the feel of her heart as it beat against his.

"So," she said, her voice muffled against his chest, "does this mean I can move my truck back in?"

"Well, yes and no."

She pulled away, her forehead creased in confusion.

"Come here, I want to show you something."

He took her hand and pulled her to the back door and out to the garage.

"Eric, what's going on?"

His heart pounded. He hoped she liked what he'd done.

"You saw how well the bakery is doing," he said, gesturing to the front sidewalk where people were steadily coming and going.

"Yes. Congratulations, it's wonderful."

"It's all you, Nat. All of it."

Her eyes widened and she shook her head, looking at the ground. He lifted her chin up, bringing her gaze back up to his. Those beautiful caramel eyes of hers were a bit misty and he smiled.

"It's all you," he repeated. "None of this would have been possible without you." He took a deep breath and went all in. "And I don't want any of it without you."

He stepped away from her and opened the doors to the garage. Inside was a brand new delivery van, painted a Tuscan red, with a brand new logo emblazoned on the side.

"Street Treats?"

Eric nodded, praying she liked it. "I combined the names of our businesses. Tuscan Treats and Street Cakes. The new sign for the building is supposed to be ready next week. I was hoping you'd join me. As a full partner. Well, as a controlling partner, actually. I'm having my lawyer draw up papers to give you a sixty percent share in the bakery."

Nat's mouth dropped open and she went around to the side of the van so she could read the logo. "Eric, I…"

"And," he said, pulling her back outside, "I've already talked to a contractor about expanding the garage. If we widened it a little, we'd be able to fit both your truck and the van inside. I want you to join me at the bakery, but I don't want you to have to give up your own business. I thought this way you could do both. If you want."

Nat stared, barely blinking, her gaze going from the truck to the bakery to him and back again. She finally walked the few feet back to the van. She looked at the logo for what felt like an eternity. Eric steeled himself against the crushing disappointment he'd feel if she said no, his fingers drumming on his leg.

"Nat?" He walked over to her, running a hand down her arm, unable to stand the suspense anymore. "It's okay if you want to say no. The garage is still yours. I can park the van on the street. I want you with me, want you to be part of this. But if you don't want—"

She turned to him, tears in her eyes, a huge smile on her face, and put her finger against his lips to shut him up. She launched herself into his arms. "Yes," she whispered.

"Yes?" he asked, hardly daring to believe all his dreams were coming true.

"Yes!" she said again, laughing. "Yes." She kissed him. "Yes." Another kiss. "Yes, yes, yes, yes."

Eric laughed with her, his heart soaring. He picked her up and spun her around. When he grew almost too dizzy to stand he put her down and kissed her again, letting his lips linger on hers until his head swam again.

Then he drew her into him with a sigh.

"Thank God you said yes," he said. "I don't know what I would have done if you'd said no. I already paid for the sign."

Nat laughed and pulled his head down for another kiss. They came up for air after a few minutes, but Nat stopped him from going back for seconds.

"Wait. Eric, your parents…"

"They'll come around. Don't worry about them." He cupped her face in his hands. "I love you, Cupcake."

Her smile lit up his world. "I love you, too, Gelato."

"Come see the inside."

He dragged her into the bakery, his heart swelling with joy and pride at the obvious admiration on her face for what he'd built.

"This is all really incredible, Eric."

"I think we should celebrate."

"Agreed. I think we could both use a treat."

"Definitely. I'll go grab the baklava."

Nat groaned and Eric laughed. "You know you love it."

"I'll plead the fifth on that one."

"Well, this one you have to try. I made it myself."

"Um…I'm not hungry."

Eric laughed. "I promise you, it's good. I hired a few bakers to take care of the other stuff because we both know no one would buy the charred mess I tend to make. But the baklava I've been working on, it's good, I promise."

He snagged a piece off the nearest tray and popped it in her mouth. She gave it a few hesitant chews and then her eyes widened in surprised delight.

"Oh my God, this is delicious!"

"Told you," he said with a grin. "Oh! One more thing to show you," he said, leading her to the front of the store so she could see the menu hanging over the counter.

"It looks wonderful," Nat said, her smile stretching from ear to ear as she took in the bustling bakery.

"I put a very special item on the menu just for you," Eric said, pointing to the lower right hand of the menu.

"The Nat Attack," Nat read. "A baker's dozen of delectable baklava."

Nat glared at him, though a smile still played on her lips. "Seriously? A baker's dozen? You named a menu item of *thirteen* pieces of baklava after me?"

Eric grinned and wrapped his arms around her. "Oh no. My baker's dozen is special."

"It is?"

He nodded. "Just like the woman it is named for. My baker's dozen is fourteen pieces," he said, leaning down to kiss her again.

Nat's laughter rang through the bakery. And nothing had ever sounded so sweet.

# Acknowledgments

My sincerest thanks to the entire Entangled team, most especially my amazing editor, Erin Molta. You have been an absolute dream come true since day one and, as always, it has been a privilege to work with you. You put the awe in awesome.

To my amazing support system, without whom I'd be a blubbering mess over in the corner: Sarah Ballance—girl… all the feels! You complete me (and I'm only sort of kidding). Toni Kerr, for everything you do for me, and all your years of support, I just can't thank you enough. Lisa, Tammi, Jodie, Jeanette—huge hugs and thanks for everything (also apologies for having to put up with me in real life).

And of course, to my sweet family who has to put up with me on a daily basis, you guys make my world go 'round.

# About the Author

Kira Archer resides in Pennsylvania with her husband, two kiddos, and far too many animals in the house. She tends to laugh at inappropriate moments, break all the rules she gives her kids (but only when they aren't looking), and would rather be reading a book than doing almost anything else. She has odd, eclectic tastes in just about everything and often let's her imagination run away with her. She loves a vast variety of genres and writes in quite a few. If you love historical romances, check out her alter ego, Michelle McLean.

*Find love in unexpected places with these satisfying Lovestruck reads...*

## DRUNK ON YOU
### a *Bourbon Boys* novel by Teri Anne Stanley

Justin Morgan would happily drown the pain of his injured leg—and the guilt he brought back from Afghanistan—in bourbon. Except, there won't *be* any booze if he doesn't rescue his family's century-old distillery from financial ruin. The problem? Allie McGrath, the youngest daughter of the distillery's co-owners and the one woman he can't have. If he can't keep their attraction under control, there's a solid chance they'll send the whole enterprise crumbling to the ground...if he doesn't crash and burn first.

## THE SEDUCTION GAME
### a novel by Emma Shortt

Millionaire bad boy, Will Thornton, is determined to buy computer-geek Kate Kelly's building out from under her. He plays the game better than anybody and charming is his middle name. Problem is, the snarky, geeky, computer-wiz is impossibly cute and a match for him in every way. Kate is prepared to wait Will out, but It'll take every ounce of her self-control to win this game. Can two such radically different people come out winners in the game of seduction?

## THE THREE-WEEK ARRANGEMENT
### a *Chase Brothers* novel by Sarah Ballance

After losing the woman he loved, Ethan Chase would rather ride solo—if his family would let him. Enter Rue Campbell, an adventure photographer literally counting the days until her plane leaves New York City. When Ethan asks her to pose as his girlfriend to get his family off his back, she figures it can't hurt. But with Ethan, there's no faking *anything*. With the sheets burning hot and the clock ticking on their arrangement, Rue's falling for a man guaranteed to derail her goals…and break her heart.

## MERGER OF THE HEART
### a *Glenwood Falls* novel by Melia Alexander

Jessica Adams just inherited the family construction business only to discover that someone has already agreed to buy it. And the big wig who made the offer is her ex-lover, Daniel Spencer… who doesn't know he's the father of her seven-year-old son. But as Daniel offers Jessica the deal of the lifetime, everything changes when he meets her son. *Their* son. Now Daniel is putting everything on the line for a new deal—*if* he can convince Jessica to take the biggest risk of her life.